SWEET SACRIFICES

A CANDLE BEACH NOVEL

NICOLE ELLIS

1

Amelia O'Connor sat on the beach, leaning against a log that had been tossed above the normal high tide mark by the fury of a winter storm, the rough bark pressing reassuringly into her back. Damp ocean air filled her lungs with every breath as she sank her bare toes into the cool sand. She lifted her camera to eye level to snap a quick photo of a seagull soaring overhead.

When she'd first arrived in Candle Beach, she hadn't known what to expect from the Washington coast. Although it was generally cooler than what she was used to in the East San Francisco Bay region, the natural beauty of the area more than made up for the need to wear a sweatshirt on summer afternoons and evenings. She'd woken this morning just after sunrise to take photos for the Candle Beach Hotel's website and had already taken close to a hundred shots of the stunning views.

She and her brother, Aidan, had been working for months to renovate the hotel, and the grand re-opening of the property the night before had been a huge success with everyone who'd attended. With any luck, the hotel would also be popular with their first overnight guests, who were scheduled to arrive the very next weekend.

They'd put everything they had into the hotel, including most of the money they'd inherited after their parents' deaths a few years prior. Not for the first time, Amelia wondered if she'd been hasty to agree to that. But they'd been talking about buying and owning a hotel together for a while, so when the historic property came on the market, Aidan had jumped at the chance to purchase it, and she'd gone alone with the plan.

However, as soon as they'd moved up to Candle Beach, Aidan had fallen in love with a local woman, Maura, and now Amelia was left feeling like a third wheel. She was happy to see her brother so happy and she genuinely liked Maura, but things were very different than how she'd imagined.

Had she jumped into the venture too fast? All of her friends were back in San Francisco and she'd given up the client base she'd worked so hard for in the six years she'd owned her own interior design business. While the idea of running a hotel had interested her, it was more Aidan's dream than hers. Giving up her life back home and moving to Candle Beach was like starting all over again.

She glanced at her watch. Almost six-thirty a.m. Although they had voicemail for non-office hours, the reservation phone lines at the hotel would officially open at eight and they'd be busy with all the publicity from the grand reopening yesterday. If she wanted time to jump in the shower and grab a bite of breakfast before work, she needed to get back. She pushed herself up from the sand and stretched the kinks out of her legs. Before leaving her favorite spot on the beach, she lifted her camera and snapped a few more shots of the surf. It seemed to change every time she looked at it, especially as the sun rose higher in the sky.

She jogged slowly back to the wooden staircase that led to the hotel, which was perched high on a cliff overlooking the Pacific Ocean. At the foot of the stairs, she stopped and took one more picture from the lower elevation, focusing in on the driftwood fort someone had constructed further down the beach. Families would enjoy seeing that on the website. She then climbed to the top and stepped out onto the path of crushed oyster shells she'd designed to wind enticingly through the grounds.

On her right, the old barn had been converted into a new museum for the Candle Beach Historical Society. It wasn't open yet for the day, but according to Maura, who volunteered there, they'd had a steady stream of visitors during the hotel's grand re-opening. Bringing the hotel back to its former glory had been important to both Amelia and her brother, so it seemed fitting to have the historical museum located on the same grounds.

As the path turned, the Candle Beach Hotel rose above her, two-plus stories of freshly painted siding, a widow's walk, and an inviting wraparound porch that the guests would love. Her chest opened with pride. She and Aidan had taken a rundown hotel that had been out of commission for over a decade and turned it into a charming beach retreat. Looking at it now, she knew their parents would be proud of what they'd accomplished with their inheritance.

She pushed open the door to the lobby and made her way back to the owner's suite she shared with her brother. Aidan was in the kitchen, blearily rubbing his eyes as he poured himself a cup of the coffee she'd brewed before heading out on her morning walk.

"Hey sis." He sipped his coffee and winced. "Ouch. They weren't joking around when they said this pot will keep the coffee hot for hours."

She laughed. "Nope. I didn't skimp on the coffee maker."

She tilted her head at the door to the lobby. "Has anyone called yet?"

He nodded his head. "A few calls, but I've let them go straight to voicemail." He eyed the lobby. "I hate not answering them, but if we're going to run this place by ourselves, we've got to set some boundaries, or it'll take over our lives." He set his coffee cup down on the counter. "Hey, I wanted to talk with you about something."

Amelia checked her watch. "Can it wait for a bit? I was hoping to get a shower in before breakfast."

He grinned. "It can wait."

When Amelia emerged from the shower twenty minutes later, the aroma of bacon and eggs hung in the air. She hastily wrapped a towel around her damp hair and dressed in a casual sundress before heading to the kitchen in the owner's suite.

"Yum. Something smells good." She filled up her cup with coffee.

Aidan grinned. "I made plenty of bacon." He set the meat on the small two-person table, next to a pan of scrambled eggs.

Amelia grabbed plates from the cupboard and forks from the drawer, then slid into a chair. "Thanks for making breakfast. I have a feeling today will be busy."

"I won't complain if it is." He shoveled a large spoonful of eggs into his mouth, then set his fork down on his plate. "So, um... What I wanted to talk to you about is Maura."

Amelia stopped crunching on a piece of bacon and stared at him. "What is it? Are you getting married?"

His face flamed as red as a tomato and he sputtered.

She stared at him. "Are you?" This was moving quicker than she'd even imagined.

"No, no. Not anytime soon at least." His cheeks paled to a calmer shade of pink. "But things are getting more serious.

We did talk a little about our future." His eyes met hers. "I think she really is 'the one'. I can't imagine my life without her now."

A wide grin spread across her lips. "I'm so happy for you. Maura's a great girl."

He nodded. "She is. I think Mom would've really liked her."

Amelia paused for a moment, retreating into her thoughts. Their mom would have adored Maura. She would have approved of her kindness, her love for children, and her ability to stand up to Aidan. She swallowed a lump in her throat. Their parents would never have the chance to see Amelia or Aidan get married or meet any future grand-children – not that there was much chance right now that Amelia would ever be providing any offspring. She'd never gotten far enough in any relationship to consider marriage or kids, so she'd have to be content with being the best auntie ever to Aidan's future children.

"You okay?" Aidan's eyes brimmed with concern.

She smiled. "Yep. Just thinking about Mom and Dad. I miss them."

"Me too," he said softly. "And these days, more than ever." He took a deep breath. "But I try to remember how much they'd love this place, and I get on with my day. Dwelling on what they're missing isn't helping with anything."

"And you've got a future with Maura to look forward to." Amelia surveyed the room. The tiny kitchen was only big enough for two. With Maura hanging around more and more, their shared living space was beginning to feel cramped. "I think it might be time for me to move out of the owner's suite."

His head reeled back. "What? Are you saying you're leaving Candle Beach? You just got here."

"No, no. Nothing like that." She patted his hand. "I was thinking that you and Maura could use some privacy. And you know me, I like my own space too. We've been sharing a house for far too long."

He frowned. "I thought things were going well."

"They are, but I'd just like a place to call my own. Don't worry. I won't go far." She looked out the small kitchen window that faced toward the road. "I was actually thinking about moving into the caretaker's cottage."

"The caretaker's cottage?" He gazed at the ceiling, his face wrinkling with thought. "I didn't have the handyman fix it up at all, besides painting it so the exterior didn't look so bad to the guests. I don't remember it being in great condition, but I haven't gone in there since we first bought the property. Getting the main building and the barn in working order were my main priorities."

"Well, how bad could it be?" Amelia finished her food and carried her dishes over to the sink to rinse them off. "I'll check it out later today and go from there, okay?"

He sighed. "I still don't like that you feel the need to leave. This is your home too."

"And it still will be," she said breezily. "I just think it's time for us to each have our own digs."

"Okay, okay." He swigged the dregs of his coffee and cleared the rest of the table. "It's a deal. But if the cottage is a mess, don't feel like you have to follow through with moving in."

She laughed. "Me? Stubbornly follow through on a poorly thought-out decision?"

"You? Never," he said with a straight face.

She slugged him in the arm as she walked past him on the way to the lobby. "Funny, funny."

In between reservation phone calls that morning, she perched on the stool behind the front desk and let her mind

6

wander. As soon as she'd told Aidan about her desire to move into the cottage, she'd felt that little surge of enthusiasm that she often got when she made a life-changing decision. Helping him to run the hotel was less exciting than she'd expected, but the cottage project would be a welcome distraction. Her moving out of the owner's suite would be a good thing for both her and Aidan.

On her lunch break, she grabbed the massive ring of miscellaneous keys from the hook under the front counter and walked outside. A warm breeze rustled the rose bushes behind the hotel, perfuming the air with their lovely scent. She'd been stuck inside for so long that it felt amazing to get out and stretch her legs. She followed the crushed shell path behind the hotel, but it ended just short of the cottage to discourage guests from investigating the building.

As she crossed the last few feet of grass to the front door of the cottage, her excitement rose. The outside of the building looked good – fresh paint and shining windows. Maybe the inside wouldn't be too bad either.

After peeking through one of the window panes next to the front door, her hopes were dashed. The cottage appeared to be stuffed with junk. She inserted the appropriately labeled key into the lock above the brass doorknob and twisted the handle. It squeaked, but the door didn't move. She pushed hard on the door and it released with a loud scraping noise.

Nothing a little TLC couldn't fix, she thought. *Maybe it won't be too bad.* She stepped inside, almost choking on dust. Someone – either their own staff or the former owners – had used the building as a storage unit. Stained mattresses, bedroom furniture, and rusted-out plumbing parts were strewn about on the cracked linoleum flooring. She pushed aside an old desk so she could move further into the room.

The action startled a mouse, who skittered across the floor and into the far corner of the living area.

This was even worse than she'd imagined. She took a deep breath of musty air, squared her shoulders and walked across the room. This time, she tried to assess it with the keen eye of an interior designer, distancing herself from any personal emotions to see the space for its possibilities.

She scanned what she could see of the main room. A small kitchen was located in one corner, complete with an ancient refrigerator and a three-burner stove. Sunlight streamed through the window over the sink and there were plenty of cupboards. Next to the kitchen were two half-open doors. The other side of the room held a small fireplace and three more windows that filled the room with light – and her soul with optimism. This could work.

She checked out the first of the two interior doors. The bedroom was tiny, but big enough to hold a full-sized bed if she was careful about her furniture choices. Like the other rooms, it had two windows divided into four panes each. This room contained less junk and she was able to cross over to the window, where a clear view of the ocean spread out in front of her, increasing her excitement.

Opening the other door revealed a bathroom with a claw-foot tub, a tile floor and a cracked sink. A strong odor of mold hung in the air and she quickly shut the door. It wasn't ideal, but the handyman Maura had helped them locate had proven quite good at fixing anything they'd thrown at him so far. He could handle getting rid of a little mold and installing new flooring and appliances. A grin tugged at the corners of her mouth.

She spun around to look back at the main room and smiled widely. This was going to work out.

2

Jordan Rivers stared at the television, his eyes locked on the images as they flashed across it, but not really seeing them. It was a romantic comedy, the type of movie that producers liked to cast him in, but not his favorite thing to watch. He used to see every new romantic comedy that came out though – Annie had loved them. If memory served him right – which it often didn't these days – they'd seen this one together while she was undergoing one of her last rounds of chemotherapy.

Man, he missed her. She'd always known how to make things better. Even when he'd spent long days on the set and felt like he couldn't move when he got home, she'd have him up and dancing in the kitchen with her, laughing as they bumped into the kitchen table.

A tear formed in the corner of his eye and he roughly brushed it away before taking a long swig from the beer bottle on the end table. There was no point in dwelling on memories of his wife. She was gone and he'd never get to dance with her again.

"Daddy?" A little girl's voice broke through his reverie.

His head shot up. What time was it anyway? There were four bottles of beer on the end table, which meant he could have been zoning out in front of the TV anywhere from one to four hours.

He swiped at his eyes again so his daughter Mia wouldn't see the remnants of tears, then looked up at her. She was wearing a two-piece pajama set festooned with a dizzying array of rainbows and unicorns. Apparently, it was somewhere around bedtime in their household.

"Hey, sweetie. Didn't Auntie Carrie put you to bed already?"

She shook her head, causing a cloud of blonde curls to float softly around her shoulders. He winced inwardly as a vision of Annie's golden locks popped into his head. When she'd talk animatedly to him about something she was passionate about, her hair would do the same as his daughter's. Even at eight years old, Mia was the spitting image of her mother.

"I brushed my teeth already." Her eyes searched his face. "Auntie Carrie said you might read to me before bed since you were home early tonight."

Early? He finally glanced at his watch. Eight-thirty. He'd been home for a little over an hour, a realization which made his stomach turn as he thought about the four beers he'd already consumed. Tomorrow. Tomorrow would be the day he'd quit drinking and be the father his daughter deserved. Tonight, he'd let himself wallow in his pain, one last time.

"Daddy's a little tired tonight, honey. I should be home in time for bedtime tomorrow. I'll read to you from one of the Narnia books, I promise." He forced a smile, which he hoped appeared genuine enough. He was an actor. This kind of stuff should come easier to him, right?

Mia wasn't fooled, and she made no effort to hide the sadness that crossed her face. "You said that last night and the night before."

"I know. I'm sorry, sweetie." A tear beaded in his left eye and he rubbed the side of his cheek to surreptitiously wipe it away. "This movie's been hard on me."

She eyed him. "Did you at least get to meet the doggy who played in that pirate movie yet?"

"Anton?" He grinned widely, not needing to act this time. Anton was a little mop of a dog, but Mia had been obsessed with him since she saw him in a movie the year before. She'd freaked out when she found out he'd be starring alongside her dad in his next movie.

She nodded, sending her curls flying again. "Did you meet him?"

"Uh-huh."

She squealed. "Can I come see him on set sometime?"

"Maybe." He looked up as someone came into the room. His sister-in-law, Carrie, stood a few feet behind Mia. "We're finishing up the movie soon, but Anton should still be around for a few more scenes. Maybe Auntie Carrie can bring you by."

Carrie shot him a dubious look as she set her hands on Mia's shoulders. "It's time for bed, honey. It looks like Daddy's a little too tired to read to you tonight."

"Oh, okay." Reluctance hung in Mia's words. "But he promised he'd read to me tomorrow night."

"I'm sure he did." Carrie eyed the row of bottles, and Jordan wished he could make them magically disappear. "Daddy's a busy man though, so we'll have to play it by ear, okay?"

"He said he'd read to me," Mia said stubbornly. "And I want to see Anton on set."

"I'll talk to Auntie Carrie about it, okay?" Jordan leaned forward to kiss his daughter's forehead, the sudden movement making his brain spin. "I'm sure Anton would love to meet you too."

"Okay, Daddy." Her tone had brightened, and she gave him a big hug in return. "Love you."

"G'night, sweetie. Love you too." He wrapped his arms around her and squeezed. She was all he had left, and he needed to figure out how to make things better for both of them. Being an actor in Hollywood had never been easy, but now with Annie gone, it was more difficult than ever.

Carrie reached for Mia's hand. "Time for bed." She led her niece across the plush carpeting in their living room and through the door to the bedroom wing of the house.

Jordan knew Carrie disapproved of his drinking, but she'd never said anything to him outright. She'd come to stay with them four years ago, when Annie had first gotten sick, and she'd been with them ever since. At that point, she'd just received her nursing license and had plans in the works to move to Florida, where his in-laws had moved after they retired ten years earlier. Instead, Carrie had stayed in Los Angeles and put aside her own dreams to first take care of Annie, then take over the role of mother to Mia – and, if he was being honest, most of the time, she was Mia's only reliable parent.

After Carrie left the room, Jordan lay back against the smooth leather pillows on the couch. How had his life gone so wrong? For a while, he'd been a golden boy – everything had gone perfectly in his life. He and Annie had met and fallen madly in love on the first weekend of their freshman year in college, had married after graduation, and had been blessed with a beautiful little girl a year later. Annie had been incredibly supportive, and they'd moved to Los

Angeles when Mia was a baby to allow him to pursue his dream of acting in the movies.

One lucky break and his career took off. Everything was perfect – until the moment in that doctor's office when their whole lives changed. Annie had encouraged him to continue pursuing his career, even if it meant time away from home – and her. He'd reluctantly taken roles far away from them, missing the chance to see Mia's first steps, dinners at home with the family, and big chunks out of the final years of his wife's life. If he could do it all again, he'd have forsaken all of the money and fame for one more night with Annie.

The soft click of a door closing down the hall alerted him that Carrie had finished putting Mia to bed. He rose quickly from the couch and snagged the four beer bottles around their long necks, quickly crossing the wide living room to the adjoining kitchen. With a practiced motion, he tossed the bottles into the recycling bin, where they clanked against the bottles he'd consumed the night before, sending a waft of stale beer into the air. One of the bottles broke into several large chunks. He sighed and gingerly grabbed the pieces, wrapping them in newspaper before throwing them in the trash. The pad of his thumb stung, and he removed a splinter of glass embedded near the joint. Blood dripped down his hand and he moved over to the sink to clean it up.

Carrie entered the kitchen, raising an eyebrow at his injury. "You okay?"

"Yeah, just a little accident." He rinsed off his hand, then wrapped it in paper towels, pressing on the wound to stop the bleeding. "Did Mia get off to bed okay?" He poured himself a cup of cold coffee and sat down at the small kitchen table.

His sister-in-law nodded. "Snoring away before I even finished the second chapter."

He smiled. "Good. She seems a little wound up lately."

Carrie eyed him, then opened and closed her mouth before pressing her lips together in a firm line.

She was hiding something.

"What?" he asked. "What is it?"

Carrie sighed. "She misses you. It's been a while since you were home early enough to have dinner with us, and even when you are home..." She walked over to the sink and ran some water over a plate before stacking it neatly in the dishwasher.

Jordan's eyes grew damp. It had been a while since he'd been there for dinner. He kept telling himself that it would just be one more long day at work, but each of those days turned into another.

"I'll do my best to be here for dinner tomorrow," he said to Carrie's back.

She turned off the sink faucet and placed two cups in the top rack of the dishwasher before turning to face him. "She needs more than an occasional visit with her dad. She misses her mom so much." She bit her lip. "I know we all miss Annie."

He looked down, focusing on the oils that swam in lazy swirls on the surface of his coffee. He missed Annie more than he'd ever thought it possible to miss another human being. "What do you think I should do? Should I quit after this role? I've socked enough away in the bank to support Mia and me, at least until she goes off to college." He raised his eyes to meet hers.

She shrugged. "I don't know what to tell you." Her eyes scanned his face and he felt his skin warm under the scrutiny. "You love what you do, right?" she asked finally.

He nodded. "I do. Acting is where I've always felt at home."

"Then keep doing it." She smiled unevenly at him and

her eyes glistened with unshed tears. "I always felt a calling to be a nurse, but my life has gone in a different direction."

Her words pierced him to the core. They had been spoken without a hint of malice or accusation, but his stomach twisted with guilt, nonetheless. He was the reason Carrie wasn't a nurse right now. He couldn't even take care of his own daughter. A little voice in his head tried to tell him he wasn't being fair to himself, but he pushed it away.

"Thank you for taking care of Mia – and me," he said quietly. "I can't even begin to repay you for it."

She waved a hand in the air. "No repayment necessary. I love Mia and I promised Annie I'd take care of her for as long as necessary." She eyed him again. "I don't want to be rude, but I have to admit – I'm a little worried about you. You're not taking care of yourself. As soon as you get home, you grab a beer from the fridge and plop down on the couch. Mia needs you to be healthy." She pulled out a ceramic mug from the cupboard and slipped a tea bag in it before filling it from the hot water spigot on the sink.

It was more like three or four beers. He stared at her. "I don't know what to do." Even to his own ears, his voice was devoid of emotion.

Carrie sat down at the table, dunking her teabag in the water the whole time. When she was satisfied with the color, she raised her eyes to meet his. "Look, I know it's not my place to say something, but Annie would have wanted you to be happy. Maybe it would help to get some time away from here – away from the pressure of being Mia's dad and away from a house full of memories of Annie. Go somewhere and get your head right so you can come home and be the dad Mia needs you to be."

Tears sprang from his eyes and he wiped them away with the back of his hand. What was going on with him? Even after Annie was diagnosed, he hadn't shed a tear. He'd stayed strong for her then, so why was he so emotional now? Was Carrie right? Did he need a break from it all?

"We're wrapping up the film next week," he said slowly. "If I make arrangements to get away for a week, would you be able to watch Mia? Maybe we can all go on vacation somewhere afterward." He felt a pang of guilt about taking advantage of Carrie's good nature and hurriedly added, "Or you can have some time off to yourself and Mia and I can go somewhere by ourselves."

She smiled and patted his hand. "We can figure that out when you get back. It's not a problem for me to watch Mia. Her summer break from school starts in two weeks, so the timing is perfect."

He sat back in his chair, feeling as though some light had entered his life. A week off to figure out what he wanted to do with his future. This felt right.

"But where would I go?" He'd never been the one to make the vacation plans. Annie had always done that. He'd just gone along with everything she'd planned for them.

Carrie smiled. "You know, I might have the perfect place for you. A good friend of mine from college is living up in Washington State, somewhere on the coast, and she's dating a guy who just opened up a small country inn. It's supposed to be gorgeous there."

A small country inn? His inner voice echoed her words and he raised his eyebrows.

She took one look at his expression and burst out laughing. "No, you won't be bored to tears. Maura loves living there, and she's used to living in bigger cities. She said the town of Candle Beach is enchanting."

"Enchanting, huh?" He took a deep breath. "Okay, what's the name of this place?"

"The Candle Beach Hotel." She grabbed her phone from her sweatshirt pocket and texted someone. "It just opened, so they may be full. I'll see if I can pull some strings and get you a room."

"Thanks, Carrie."

The evening had started out on a glum note, but things were looking up. Maybe this Candle Beach Hotel would be just what he needed to get his life back on track.

3

_____

"The downstairs rooms are done," Amelia called out as she heaved the cleaning cart across the threshold between the guest room hallway and the lobby of the Candle Beach Hotel. It caught on the lip of the lobby's hardwood floor, but a final push got it over the hump. "I'll get started on the upstairs after I take a break for some coffee. Cleaning rooms is no joke. I feel like I've just run a marathon." She leaned down to straighten some bottles of disinfectant that had toppled over. "People are such slobs though. You wouldn't believe what I've seen in some of those rooms. One of them had so much sand on the sheets that you could make a castle out of it."

From behind the front desk, Aidan cleared his throat. "Amelia?"

Amelia wiped her arm over her forehead to mop away some sweat and looked up from the cart. On the other side of the desk from her brother was the most handsome man she'd ever seen in real life – like a modern-day Clark Gable. She'd watched Gone with the Wind so many times that the DVD was threatening to give out, but she was pretty sure she wasn't imagining this man. The dark sunglasses the mystery man wore only added to his allure.

"Oh. I didn't realize you were with a guest." Heat shot up her neck and spread to her cheeks as she attempted to rip the hideous yellow rubber gloves off of her hands. No matter how hard she pulled on the left glove, it clung to her skin like it had been glued on. She glanced up to see the man staring at her. The dark grey lenses hid his eyes, but a smile danced across his lips. Time stood still as she died a slow death from embarrassment. She tugged harder on the rubber fingertips – then watched in horror as it suddenly gave way and flew across the room, bouncing harmlessly off the guest's shoes.

Amelia gave Aidan a furtive glance, but his lips were pressed tightly together like he was trying hard not to laugh.

The guest bent down, plucked the glove from the floor, then walked over to her. He smiled and held it out. "I can never get these things off either."

Her face must have been as red as the roses on the counter by now. She took the glove from him and tossed it into the cart, then smoothed the maid's uniform she'd changed into to protect her normal work clothes, took a steadying breath, and met the man's gaze. With a forced smile, she said, "Welcome to the Candle Beach Hotel. Sorry for interrupting your conversation."

He grinned at her, revealing a row of perfectly straight, pearly-white teeth. "No worries. I was just getting checked in here, but I think I'm almost done." He glanced at Aidan.

Aidan looked past the man to smirk at Amelia, then held out a key card to the man. "And you have amazing timing. I hear your room has just been cleaned."

At this moment, Amelia would have given anything to disappear into the floor.

The man plucked the key out of Aidan's hand, flipping it

between well-manicured fingers. "Excellent." He turned to Amelia and said, "I wouldn't mind a sandcastle in my room. We are at the beach after all." He winked at her and disappeared down the guest hall, towing a large rolling suitcase topped by a carry-on sized briefcase.

He was handsome and nice to boot. And now he thought she was an idiot.

Amelia groaned. "I'm so embarrassed! I can't believe he heard me complaining about another guest." She leaned against the front desk. "Why did you let me keep talking? Now we'll probably get a horrible review on Yelp."

Aidan's lips twisted with mirth. "I didn't get a chance to get a word in edgewise. Once you get started, you're kind of a motormouth."

She glared at him. "Yeah, well, next time you're stuck cleaning the guest rooms and I'm manning the front desk. Seriously, some of those rooms were pretty gross."

He held up a finger. "Actually, I've got some good news for you on that front. We received two new applications for the housekeeping position today." He retrieved a few pieces of paper from behind the desk and held them up in front of her.

She grabbed the applications from him. "I'll give them a call this afternoon and set up some interviews."

"Thanks." The phone rang and Aidan reached for it.

Amelia glanced briefly at the forms Aidan had given her. Both applicants had prior housekeeping experience. Thank goodness. In the last few days, she'd learned just how hard their job could be. The next time she stayed in a hotel, she planned to leave the cleaning staff a huge tip. The full-time housekeeper they'd hired had quit after only a few days of work and the two of them had been stuck cleaning all of the rooms along with managing the hotel. She'd expected long hours as they got the hotel up and running, but this was ridiculous.

Amelia rolled the cart into the owner's suite and poured herself a cup of leftover coffee. Aidan had left the pot on and it was still warm. When she'd drank the last drop, she reluctantly got back to work. Unfortunately, those hotel rooms weren't going to clean themselves.

After her evening shift at the desk, Amelia locked up the computer and put everything away. She gave the hotel lobby a quick sweep so it would be fresh and clean for the next morning and refilled the rack of brochures for local attractions. Aidan had gone out on a date with Maura and Amelia didn't expect him back until later, so she had the owner's suite to herself. It was the perfect time for a big bowl of buttered popcorn and the new black-and-white movie she'd found on eBay. Aidan liked to make fun of her love of old movies, so she tried to take advantage of using the TV while he was out.

The handyman had started renovations on the caretaker's cottage, but it would be a week or two before it would be ready for her to move in. Her stomach jumped at the thought of having her own place after sharing a home with her brother for so long. She couldn't wait to put her own touch on the space. Even when she'd lived on her own in San Francisco, she'd always rented an apartment and hadn't been able to choose her own paint colors or anything else that altered the space in a semi-permanent manner. Being an interior decorator, this had grated on her nerves. The cottage would be her opportunity to have something in Candle Beach that was truly hers.

She went outside to check on the deck furniture,

straightening the tables and chairs as she walked along the long deck facing the ocean. When they were ready for the next day, lined up like neat rows of soldiers, she stepped off of the deck and eyed the hotel. Highlighted by the moonlight, it was elegant and charming – exactly as they'd intended. Behind her, the ocean roared, and a breeze ruffled her hair. She sniffed the air – cool and crisp. The perfect kind of evening for a solo beach walk.

But Aidan was out, and she was the manager on duty. She glanced at the lobby door. What were the odds that someone would need her at this time of night? Besides, their cell phone numbers were listed prominently next to the front desk. If she stayed on the beach close to the stairs to the hotel, she could be back in a jiffy if she got called to the desk.

That decided, she crossed the well-manicured lawn to the beach access. Next to it, the gazebo stood sentry, lit up with white twinkly lights. They'd also hung a blue lantern at the top of the stairs to the beach. Without something as a guide, it was near impossible to find the path back to the hotel in the dark, when every part of the beach looked the same.

She picked her way down the stairs and stepped out onto the cool sand. It filtered softly through her sandals, tickling her toes. She inhaled deeply. Although she'd always liked being near the water, she'd never realized how much she'd love living at the beach or how quickly it would become part of her soul. Candle Beach had only been home for a couple of weeks, but she had a hard time remembering what it was like to live anywhere else.

The beach stretched out in front of her, illuminated only by the moon shining on the surf. From experience, she knew her eyes would adjust to the darkness in a few minutes. When she felt comfortable venturing off the path, she made her way over to her favorite pile of driftwood, a few hundred feet from the stairs to the hotel. With familiarity, she climbed over the first log to reach the place where she liked to sit, but her foot caught on a strange object and she tumbled forward. She reached out to catch herself, but only succeeded in scraping her hand on rough bark before landing on soft-packed sand.

A shadowy figure shot up from the darkness and said in a deep voice, "I'm so sorry. I didn't see you coming. I think I accidentally tripped you with my foot."

She rolled over on her side, quickly coming to a seated position against a beach log and looked up at the man. Pain seared across the skin of her injured palm, causing her to wince. "I didn't see you either."

He shone a flashlight in her direction, blinding her for a moment. "Did you get hurt? Are you okay?"

"I don't know." She eyed her hand. "I think I banged it up when I fell."

He moved closer and focused the flashlight on her injury. A patch of skin had been scraped, but it wasn't bleeding. "Can you move it?"

She flexed and released the muscles in her fingers. It hurt, but nothing was broken except maybe her pride. Her eyes finally adjusted to the dark and his features became clearer. She sucked in her breath. It was the man from the hotel, the handsome guy who'd reminded her of Clark Gable.

"I think it's just a flesh wound." She took a step back. "I think I'm fine."

He reached for her palm. "Well, better let me check and make sure. Can you shine this on your hand please?" He held the flashlight out to her.

"Are you a doctor?" She took the flashlight and positioned it so he could see.

"No, but I played one on TV," he joked as he reached for her hand, enveloping it between his strong fingers.

She smiled weakly at him through the pain. "Well, you have a wonderful bedside manner."

"Why thank you." He grinned at her as he palpated her wrist, his touch so gentle and caring that she almost forgot why he was doing it. "I think it's just the scrape."

He continued to hold on to her hand, sending tingles up and down her arm that had nothing to do with her injury. She couldn't take her eyes off of his fingers encircling her wrist.

He took a closer look at her and released her hand. "Hey, you're the woman from the hotel – Amelia, right?"

She sighed. "Yep, that's me." She must have made quite an impression on him earlier, and probably not in a good way. She peered at him, trying to see if he remembered how inappropriately she'd acted earlier. His eyes held nothing but a touch of sadness.

"Well, my room is very clean. You're great at your job." He gave her a warm but lopsided grin. "I'm Jordan, by the way."

"I'm not—" She started to say that she wasn't a maid, but after her embarrassing gaffe earlier that day, she was probably better off not having him know that she was a co-owner of the hotel. "Uh, thank you."

"You're welcome." He flicked off the flashlight. "The hotel is one of the finest I've ever stayed in."

"Thank you." As soon as she said it, she felt like an idiot. She'd just thanked him two times in less than thirty seconds. There was something about this man that made her act like a teenager talking to her crush for the first time. She couldn't see him clearly in the darkness, but she could feel his presence and every nerve in her body was on high alert. How was he having this effect on her?

"I'd better go," she whispered.

He reached out and rested his hand on her arm. "No, please don't. I'll leave. I've been out here for a while and this is obviously somewhere you like to sit." He stood and stepped back a few feet.

"No, you stay. I live here year-round. You're a guest." She rotated her wrist and pushed herself off the ground with her good hand.

"It's a beautiful night," he said, almost as though he didn't want her to go. "Is it always like this?"

She paused. "Not always. It rains a lot. But on nice clear days, yeah. This is what the evenings are like." She gazed out at the moonlit ocean. "Peaceful."

"Have you lived in Candle Beach for a long time?" He moved closer to her.

She turned back to him. Ordinarily, she'd be a little concerned about being alone on a deserted beach at night with a stranger, but something about him put her at ease. Maybe it was how kind he'd been to her earlier at the hotel when she'd acted like an idiot, or perhaps it was the hint of sadness she'd caught in his eyes when he was checking her for injuries.

She laughed nervously. "No, actually I just moved up here about two months ago."

He tilted his head to the side. "For the job?"

She froze. She had moved up here for a job, in a sense, just not the housekeeping job he was referring to. "Kind of. I'd been living in the Bay Area for most of my life, but after I lost my parents suddenly a couple of years ago, I started thinking maybe it was time for a change. There were just too many things there that reminded me of them."

He stared at her. Had she said too much? Until she said it to him, she hadn't even realized that it was true — living in the Bay Area was a constant reminder of the loss of her parents and the move to Candle Beach had lessened the pain of losing them. Still though, she didn't need to tell a guest her life story less than twenty-four hours after meeting them.

Aidan always said she jumped into things without thinking, although she preferred to think of herself as being an open book. Keeping secrets wasn't her thing. Then again, she'd let this guest think she was a maid, so honesty wasn't her best trait at the moment.

"I'm sorry," she said in a rush. "Sometimes I overshare."

"No." He searched her face. "I appreciate the honesty."

Her stomach twinged and her face flamed. Aidan often teased her about how terrible she was at lying. Thank goodness it was so dark, or Jordan would know she wasn't being completely truthful.

He stepped on a log with gnarled burrs on its side, then climbed to a higher on before lowering himself to a seated position. He stared out to sea for a moment, then took a deep breath and faced her. "I know what you're going through. I lost my wife a couple of years ago."

She eased herself onto a log across from him. "I'm so sorry for your loss."

He nodded. "It hasn't been easy. I miss her more than anything."

His words were so choked up that she could feel the pain radiating from him. She fought for the right words of comfort, but ended up lamely asking, "Had you been married long?"

"About eight years, but we were together for four years before that, and we have a beautiful daughter together." He smiled. "We were college sweethearts." He rubbed his eyes with the back of his hand. "I'm sorry to lay all of this on you. Maybe I'm an oversharer too."

"Don't even worry about it." She smiled back at him.

"There's something spiritual about being out here at night when it's so quiet. Anytime there's something on my mind, I come to this spot to think."

"That must be it." He rubbed his thumb over the sun- and sand-roughened tree trunk next to him, then his eyes met hers. "I haven't talked about Annie with anyone."

"Annie was your wife?" she asked.

He nodded again. "Yes. She would have loved this." He swept his hand through the air, gesturing at the long, empty stretch of beach. "Oh, man. I think this is the first time since she died that I haven't thought of her and felt like throwing up."

"Uh..."

He laughed. "No, that's a good thing. Maybe my sister-in-law, Carrie, was right. A vacation in Candle Beach was exactly what I needed."

"Well, good," she said warmly. "That's what we hope for with all of our guests. You should come back and bring your daughter with you. We have a ton of stuff here for kids to do." She knew how hard losing her own parents had been, but she couldn't imagine what it would have been like to lose them at such a young age. And being a single father couldn't be easy either.

He smiled again. "Maybe I will bring Mia here some-time. I think she'd enjoy it." He cocked his head to the side. "You must really love working at the hotel. You sound very invested in it."

"I guess I am," she said truthfully. "It's such a gorgeous building with so much history. Did you know it opened in the early 1900s? Back in the day, it was famous as a wedding and honeymoon destination." She stopped, wanting to eat her words. Jordan had just told her about losing his wife, and then she'd blathered on about happy couples enjoying their time at the hotel.

"It sounds amazing – like something straight out of that old movie, The Beach Hotel." He sounded glad that she'd inadvertently changed the subject.

She felt her eyes widen. "You've seen The Beach Hotel?"

"Of course. It's only the best black-and-white movie ever made."

"I don't know about the best, but it's right up there in my top favorites." She sighed. "They just don't make movies like that anymore. My brother thinks I'm crazy, but I have a collection of over fifty old black-and-white movies. Some of them are getting hard to find though. I've been looking all over for one that a friend recommended to me."

He laughed. "I don't think that's crazy at all. I love them too." He tilted his head to the side. "What's the one your friend recommended? Maybe I've seen it."

"It's called Daisy's Choice. I don't think there are many copies still in existence, but my friend said it's wonderful."

"Hmm. I don't think I've heard of that one. I'll have to look it up." He shifted on the log. "Have you seen The Grand Party?"

"Nope. Is it good?"

He laughed. "I wouldn't say it was the best movie ever, but it was pretty funny."

They compared their favorite old movies and then the conversation turned to famous places they'd visited, followed by a hodgepodge of random topics. Talking to him was easy and he seemed to like being with her as well.

After a while, she shivered and pulled her sweatshirt tight against her body. Every part of her was going numb from the chilly temperature or from sitting on the hard log, but she was enjoying Jordan's company so much that she didn't want to leave.

He stopped talking. "Are you cold?" He tapped his wrist and his watch glowed. "It's past midnight!"

"Seriously?" She checked her own watch. He was right. "We've been talking for hours."

He jumped down from his perch and reached for her uninjured hand, covering it with his own. "So we have. You're freezing. Did you leave your car at the hotel? I'll walk you back."

She nodded. "My car is at the hotel." Her heart was hammering. Should she tell him that she owned the hotel with her brother and that she lived on the premises? She hated not telling him the truth. But, in all likelihood, he wouldn't be at the hotel much longer, so was it worth the risk that he'd be upset with her for lying? At this point, she felt confident that he wasn't going to leave a bad review because of her inappropriate behavior, but he'd pointed out how much he appreciated her honesty.

Before she could reach a decision, he helped her down to the ground. They climbed across the tangled mass of logs until they reached the open beach. The tide had come in and the waves now lapped at the sand only twenty feet from where they'd been sitting.

"Does the tide come up to where we were?" His eyes were fixed on the surf.

She shook her head. "Not in the summer. But friends of mine who have lived here for a long time told me that Candle Beach gets some fierce winter storms." She pointed behind them. "The winds and winter tides force the drift-wood high on the beach. It's actually pretty dangerous to be down here during a storm because the logs can roll unpredictably."

He whistled. "That's impressive. It's hard to picture right now with the waves so calm, but I'd love to be here in the winter to see it."

Her stomach flip-flopped at the thought of him being there in the winter. She pushed the thought out of her mind.

He was a temporary guest of the hotel and had a life to go back to somewhere else. With a start, she realized she'd never asked him where he called home.

"Do you live near the ocean at home?" she asked.

"No, not really. I live near Los Angeles, but more toward the mountains than the ocean." He uttered a low laugh. "I think it's been years since I've been to the beach."

"Really? I always think of L.A. as being a big beach town." She motioned up at the blue light at the top of the cliff. "That's the hotel up there."

"Oh, good. I was hoping you knew the way back. I didn't realize how dark it would be when I came down. Everything looks the same."

They turned toward the path through the beach grass that led to the hotel. Amelia's feet dragged in the soft sand as they approached the stairs. She didn't want this night to end. Too soon though, they reached the manicured grass lawn that marked the boundary of the hotel grounds. As they neared the main building, Amelia eyed her car in the parking lot.

"My car's just right over there," she said. "You don't have to walk me the whole way."

"I don't mind," he said with an easy grin.

"I'll be fine." She pressed her lips together and jutted out her chin. She only had to keep up this charade for a little longer. Her brain screamed at her that she was making a big mistake.

He put his hands up in the air. "Okay, okay. I guess I'm used to L.A. where it's not always safe to walk around alone at night." He gave her the now familiar lopsided grin.

She relaxed her expression and laughed. "It takes some getting used to."

He cleared his throat. "Speaking of the local area, I'm only in town for a few more days. Do you think you might be able to show me around a little before I leave? Maybe after you're off work tomorrow?"

She froze in place. A few more days of pretending to be a hotel maid couldn't hurt, right? Before she could overanalyze things, she said, "Sure. I'll meet you outside of the lobby tomorrow at five o'clock. Does that sound okay?"

"It sounds perfect." He started to walk toward the lobby entrance, then turned back to her. "Amelia?"

"Yeah?" She thought her heart was going to jump out of her chest.

"I had a nice time with you tonight." His eyes searched her face, as if hoping his feelings were reciprocated.

They were.

"Me too." She smiled at him and the relief in his eyes made her insides melt.

"I'll see you tomorrow." He smiled back at her, then entered the hotel.

She stayed there for a minute, watching him disappear before she crossed the lawn to the back of the hotel and the exterior entrance to the owner's suite. Her brother's bedroom door was closed, so he must be back from his date with Maura. Luckily, he wasn't awake to see how giddy she was from spending time with Jordan, or she'd never live it down. She quietly got ready for bed and fell asleep, still smiling.

4

The sun shining through the open window of his hotel room woke Jordan the next morning. Before he'd gone to bed, he'd slid the window up in its wood frame to allow the fresh ocean air to enter the room. Now, it was filled not only with that fresh air, but also a golden yellow light and the sounds of songbirds and seagulls flying past outside. Further away, the surf roared as it crashed onto the beach. Candle Beach relaxed him more than anywhere he'd ever been. Maybe Amelia was right about this place being almost magical.

Amelia. He'd returned to his room last night walking on air and feeling as though the crack left behind by Annie's death had started to heal. Carrie's theory – that being away from all of his memories could help him – had panned out. He had a lot of work to do though, and he wasn't sure where Amelia fit into all of it – that is, if she was even interested in him. She hadn't reacted like most people did when she met him, so he didn't think she recognized him – not something he was accustomed to. Her lack of recognition was refreshing, and probably why he'd felt like he could be honest with her. He'd met way too many women who were awed by his fame and money and couldn't care less about who he really was inside.

From the moment Amelia walked into the hotel lobby the morning before, her sass and energy had made him feel alive. He'd never expected to meet her again though, or to spend hours talking to her on the beach. Then again, a lot of things in his life hadn't gone according to plan. *I suppose I'll see how things go tonight,* he thought.

He glanced at the nightstand. Whoever furnished this room had worked hard to make it look like it had when the hotel first opened back in the early 1900s. Even the state-of-the-art alarm clock was enclosed in an old-fashioned wooden case. It read six-thirty a.m. His tour of town – or was it a date? – with Amelia was a long way off.

He rolled over and looked out the window. From his third-floor room, he could see all the way to the majestic blue rolling waves of the Pacific Ocean. Why hadn't he bought a house on the ocean like other actors had? It hadn't been for lack of money, but he and Annie had wanted to raise Mia with a simpler life in hopes that she wouldn't turn out like so many other children of stars did.

At least they'd succeeded with that. In his completely unbiased opinion, Mia was a likeable, well-adjusted kid. Well, as much as any kid could be who'd lost her mother two years prior. According to Carrie, she was doing well in school and had a lot of friends.

He got up and walked closer to the window, breathing in the damp, salty air. From outside came the sounds of other guests on the covered patio below his room, their coffee cups clinking as they set them down on a hard surface. Breakfast sounded good, and from what Aidan had told him when he checked in, the scones and other pastries the hotel brought in for breakfast from the local café were excellent.

His stomach grumbled and he dressed quickly in a casual polo shirt and khaki shorts.

After getting his coffee and a cherry Danish from the continental breakfast set up in the Great Room, he lucked out and found a spare chair on the deck to sit in. He'd hoped to catch a glimpse of Amelia, but he didn't see her in any of the common rooms. He sipped his coffee and gazed at the view, then bit into the Danish, cherry oozing out onto his chin. He wiped his face and admired the pastry. Aidan had been right. They were excellent. Most bakeries only used a tiny dollop of filling, but no one could complain about how much of the fresh cherry filling this baker had used.

He quickly finished the pastry but savored the last few drops of coffee. The day stretched out before him, long and empty. He wasn't sure whether he liked the possibilities that such a day offered or if it was a welcomed change from his normal schedule. He eyed the ocean and beach below. The weather was still cool, and it had been a while since he'd been out for a long run outside.

Although time was usually at a premium, he had to maintain his physique if he wanted to continue getting roles as a leading man. He managed to squeeze in an hour of cardio and weight training most days of the week, but he hated it the whole time. Maybe the next role he took should be one where he'd get to gain thirty pounds. His lips twitched with mirth at the thought of eating nothing but junk food. Whatever the case, a run today would take up time and qualify as what Carrie considered a healthy habit.

He changed into exercise clothes and running shoes, then stretched lightly before jogging down the stairs, taking them two at a time. As he passed the second-floor landing, he caught a glimpse of someone who looked like Amelia, but she was at the far end of the hallway and he didn't want to bother her while she was working. Still, the possible sighting sent a little thrill running through him. He bounced down the rest of the steps and gave Aidan a wave as he went past the front desk and out the front door.

He usually liked to listen to music as he ran on the treadmill, mainly to help with the boredom, but today he allowed his ears to remain unfettered, listening to the soundtrack of nature. He passed a few guests who were playing croquet on the lawn and slowed a little as he made his way down the steps to the beach. At this time of the morning, not many people were down there yet, and he felt as though he had the whole stretch to himself.

His thoughts wandered in and out of everything pressing on his mind. His agent had e-mailed him about a few new roles to consider and he'd told Carrie he'd think about whether or not he wanted to stay in the acting business. Was taking on a role in a new movie what he wanted? His last job had left him stressed out and borderline depressed. He couldn't continue like that.

Whatever the case, he knew he wanted some time to spend with Mia. She deserved that from him. He ran faster, thinking about his daughter. It had seemed selfish to take this time off to himself, but he knew it had been the right choice. He needed to get his head straight before making any major decisions about his future.

But where did Amelia fit in? He'd only met her yesterday and she was already a fixture in his mind. Should he be thinking about dating? Was this a possibility for a real relationship, or was it just a fling? He winced. He didn't think he was capable of a casual fling and Amelia didn't seem like that type of girl either.

Since Annie's death and even before, the media often linked him to other women, usually other celebrities. The tabloids liked to surmise that he was a real Romeo because he sometimes played one on screen. Nothing could be further from the truth. Other than one casual girlfriend in high school, it had always been Annie for him. She'd always laughed when tabloids reported that he'd been seen with another woman because she'd known she could trust him.

After her death, the rumors had intensified. He'd tried not to fan the flames by objecting to the media's claims, but he worried Mia would catch wind of them. He wasn't sure how she'd react to news of him dating someone other than her mom, even if it wasn't true.

He ran until he was exhausted, then climbed the stairs to the hotel, relishing the warmth and limberness in his leg muscles. Most of the breakfast crowd had cleared as he passed the wide covered porch. When he reached his room, he showered, then sat down on the bed, staring at his phone. It was Saturday and Mia would be home. He wanted to talk to her, but as he sat there, he realized he had no idea what to say to her. It had been so long since they'd had a real conversation, just the two of them.

He forced himself to press the call button.

Carrie answered after two rings. "Hey, how's it going? Is it nice up there?"

"It's great. The hotel is as beautiful as you told me it would be – maybe even nicer. It's not a five-star resort, but it's got its own special qualities. And it's right on the ocean. You wouldn't believe the view I have from my room." He cast a glance outside, admiring the stretch of beach he'd just run along.

"I'll bet. I'd love to see it sometime. It's been ages since I had a real vacation." Her tone was wistful, and guilt panged in his chest. He was up here enjoying a quiet vacation alone and she was back home, taking care of his daughter.

"I'll make sure you get a chance to see it. I bet you'd have a great time connecting back up with your friend."

"It's been years since I saw Maura. I'd love to visit her."

She muffled the phone, but he could still hear her talking to someone. "It's Daddy. Do you want to talk to him?"

He couldn't hear his daughter's response. "Is that Mia? Can I talk to her?"

"It is. Let me hand the phone over." Carrie went quiet.

"Daddy?" Mia's little voice came over the phone line, high and youthful.

"Yes, honey, it's me. How was school yesterday?" When he'd left for the airport the day before, she'd still been in bed.

"It was good. Jamie was out sick. I can't believe she was sick on the last Friday of the school year." She was so indignant about it that he couldn't help but chuckle. He felt a little twinge upon realizing that he had no clue who Jamie even was. Apparently, she was an important part of his daughter's life, but he'd never even heard of her before.

"Sorry, honey." He cleared his throat. "Are you looking forward to school being over?"

"Yeah!" she said with exuberance. "Are we going on a trip when school's out? Maybe to Disneyland? Jamie got to go to Disneyland for Spring Break. I really wanted to go."

"Maybe." He hadn't made any plans yet for where they'd go when he got back home, and she was out of school. Finalizing arrangements to come to Candle Beach had been the furthest he'd thought ahead. "It's a possibility."

"Awesome!"

He pictured the excitement on his daughter's face and shook his head, but he couldn't help grinning.

"I'm so excited, Daddy!" The words bubbled across the line.

"Me too." He closed his eyes for a moment, imagining the two of them riding on a roller coaster together and meeting some of the Disney characters. He and Annie had gone to Disneyland when they'd first moved out to Los

Angeles and they'd always intended to take Mia there, but life had gotten crazy and a family trip to Disneyland had been the furthest thing from either of their minds.

"Are you still there, Daddy?" she asked, sounding unsure of herself.

"I'm here. Just thinking about you meeting Mickey for the first time."

"I want to meet Cinderella and Sleeping Beauty too," she said. "And Jamie got to go to a beauty parlor and get her hair done and her mommy bought her a tiara!"

A tiara? Sheesh. This parenting-a-girl thing was harder than he'd imagined. "We'll see about the tiara and the beauty parlor." The words felt odd coming off his tongue. He'd been depending on Carrie to take care of Mia's needs, but he hadn't realized how much of his daughter's life he'd been missing. The last he knew, she'd been playing in the dirt and making forts in the backyard. Now she wanted to meet Disney princesses.

"Okay." Disappointment hung in her voice. "But I want to at least meet Cinderella."

"I'm sure we can make that happen." He hoped he wouldn't let her down on his promise. Usually when he went out in public, he wore huge sunglasses and a hat to avoid the public eye, but if he needed to, he was willing to pull out the celebrity card to have his daughter fulfill her wish of meeting Cinderella.

"Mia," Carrie's voice called out. "We've got to leave for swim lessons. Tell Daddy goodbye and go change into your swimsuit."

"Okay, Aunt Carrie," Mia said away from the phone. Her voice then came back clearer. "I've got to go to swimming. Are you going to call me later?"

"Maybe tomorrow. I miss you, honey."

"I miss you too, Daddy. I'm so excited about going to Disneyland though. I can't wait until you come home."

"Me too." He swallowed a lump in his throat. "Bye."

Carrie's voice came back on the line. "Sorry, Jordan, but she already missed last week's swim lesson because she was at a friend's house. I don't want her to miss this one too."

"No problem. I understand." He stared out the window. His throat still felt tight. "Thank you for taking such good care of her."

She laughed. "Of course. Don't worry about it. I hope you're enjoying your time up there. Relax a little, get some rest. We'll be here when you get back."

"Thanks, Carrie. I appreciate it. I'll call again tomorrow." He pushed "End Call" on his phone and watched as it returned to his background – a picture of him, Annie and Mia, laughing together at a park. Tears came to his eyes. If only he could get that back.

He heard a noise in the hallway, which startled him out of his memories and reminded him of Amelia. He took a deep breath. He couldn't get the past back, but it was time to start looking toward the future.

5

"Do you mind working the front desk by yourself today?" Amelia asked. "I'm interviewing house-keepers and then I need to take care of some other business stuff."

Aidan took his eyes off the computer screen and looked up at her. "Sure. Did you get interviews scheduled with both of the women who applied for the job?"

"Yep. And one who e-mailed me an application. There has to be one reliable applicant out of the three."

"Maybe even two." He smiled at her. "Dana's working today though, right?"

She nodded. "Yep. She agreed to take on another shift this week, but she can't do it most weeks because of her kids' schedules."

He frowned. "That's too bad. She's such a good worker." He laughed. "Lots better than you are. I doubt she'd ever complain about other guests in front of a guest like you did. Although, I think that guy took it better than most would."

Her face flamed as she glared at him. "I said I was sorry. I don't know what came over me. I don't think he was too upset though." Butterflies danced in her stomach as she thought about Jordan's reaction and their unplanned meeting on the beach. He'd been the consummate gentleman and hadn't even mentioned her bad behavior once last night.

"He seems like an easygoing sort of guy." His eyes scanned her face and that funny smile crossed his lips, like it always did when he was hiding something from her.

"What?" she asked.

"Nothing." His eyes twinkled as he proclaimed his innocence. "I was thinking about how he reacted."

"Ugh." Thank goodness she'd let him think she was the maid. If she could only get through showing him around town that evening, she'd be safe.

A guest came downstairs and passed the desk as they made their way into the Great Room. Amelia's eyes darted around. Jordan could come downstairs anytime, and it wouldn't be good if he saw her dressed in normal clothes, hanging out in the lobby.

"I've got to go." She gestured at their office off the lobby. "When the applicants for the housekeeper job arrive, can you please send them in to me?"

"Sure, sure. Leave me to do all the hard work."

She stared at him. Was he serious?

His lips quivered with a poorly suppressed smile. "I'm joking. Go take care of business."

"Thanks." She disappeared into the office and shut the door behind her, collapsing into the ergonomic desk chair. She was learning more and more that she didn't have the same passion for the business that Aidan did. He lived and breathed the hospitality industry. If it weren't for Maura, Amelia was pretty sure that he'd spend all of his time at the hotel, figuring out how to make it absolutely perfect.

It hadn't been a complete fabrication – she did have work to do. It just wasn't urgent. After she finished her work and interviewed the three housekeeping applicants, one after another, she logged off the computer. Before opening the office door, she peeked into the lobby.

To her chagrin, when she opened the door, Aidan happened to be facing her direction as he watched a document come out of the printer.

He raised his left eyebrow. "Why do you look like you're in some sort of spy movie?"

For the second time that day, she felt the telltale flush work its way up her neck. "I, uh, didn't want to startle you if you were deep in work."

He gave her a dubious look. "Okay..."

"Do you mind if I head out to lunch with my friends?"

"Sure. How did the interviews go? Any likely candidates?"

She nodded. "I hired the second woman who came in. The others sounded good too, but I really liked the second woman. She starts tomorrow."

He whistled loudly. "Way to go. Getting things done. I hope I have as much luck with an on-call handyman. Elvis is great, but he's not able to come out at all hours of the day or night."

"Plus, he's busy with my cottage." She grinned at him. "It should be done in the next week or so and then I'll be out of your hair."

He sighed. "You're not bothering me. We're in this together, so we should share the owner's suite."

"Uh-huh. Anyway, I'd better get going. I promised the girls I'd meet them at the wine bar at noon."

"Can you bring me back one of those chicken salads I like?" He gave her a sad puppy-dog look. "I've been starving all day."

"You had breakfast three hours ago. I saw you mow through four of the leftover pastries. You couldn't possibly be hungry!" She smiled. It was nice to see her brother so happy. He'd finally achieved his dream of hotel ownership and was in a relationship with a great woman. In the space of a few months, his whole life had turned around. She could only hope that she'd have the same good fortune.

"Chicken salad," he said sternly.

"Aye, aye, Captain." She saluted him and then marched out the door into the sunlight.

~

When Amelia entered Off the Vine, several of her friends were already seated at the large booth in the corner. She waved at them and crossed the room.

"I can move, just give me a few seconds," Maggie said from the chair she was sitting in at the open part of the booth. She scooted the chair over, huffing and puffing as she did. "My belly is too big to slide into the booth anymore. Thank goodness Dahlia isn't coming today or we'd be squished here at the end. I know she's as anxious as I am for these little ones to make their entrance into the world."

Amelia laughed and slid into the booth. "Well, you look great, even if you can't fit into a booth right now. You've got that pregnant glow."

"I think that's sweat, not glow," Maggie grumbled as she moved her chair back to its original position. "Being nine months pregnant in the summer was not my best idea."

"It'll all be worth it when your little girl arrives," Charlotte said. "I can't wait to spoil her."

Maggie gave them grateful looks. "I know. I just feel like a grouchy whale right now. I keep reminding myself that this doesn't last forever."

The waitress came by and handed menus to Maggie, Gretchen, Charlotte, Maura and Amelia. Amelia read through the menu, even though she already knew what she was going to have – the maple chicken salad with glazed pecans. Like Aidan, she was obsessed with it and got it every time she went to the wine bar. For such a small town, Candle Beach had a surprising number of excellent restaurants, including the one Maggie owned, the Bluebonnet Café, where they bought the morning pastries for the hotel.

After the waitress took their lunch orders, Maura looked across the table at Amelia. "How are things going at the hotel? Aidan seems pretty happy with everything, but I've been wondering how you were doing."

"Things are fine." Amelia unrolled the silverware from the paper napkin in front of her. With Maura dating Aidan, she didn't want to tell her that working at the hotel wasn't as fulfilling as she hoped it would be.

"Just fine?" Gretchen asked. "I'd have thought you'd be walking on air right now. Everyone's talking about how amazing the grand re-opening of the hotel was."

Charlotte peered at Amelia. "I bet now that the design phase is over, she misses the creative aspect of it. Right?"

Amelia felt a rush of gratitude flow through her. As a talented artist, Charlotte understood how much she missed her interior design career. They'd grown close over the last few weeks as they worked together to find the best combinations of Charlotte's art, and several of her paintings of local scenery now hung on the walls of the hotel.

"I do miss it." Amelia pulled the napkin into her lap and twisted it until the fibers separated and tore. She eased her grip on it and folded her hands in front of her on the table. "I thought I'd love helping Aidan run the hotel, but sometimes it feels as though it's not a good fit for me."

"Oh, I'm sure you're doing a wonderful job," Maura said. "Aidan tells me almost every day how much he appreciates your support."

Although Maura had intended for her words to comfort, they twisted the knife a little deeper. Aidan needed her. She couldn't even consider quitting on him now. Amelia took a deep breath and smiled at Maura.

"Well, I love working with him." That much was true. Her brother was usually easy to work for, but that was the problem – she essentially worked for him as he managed most of the hotel operations. She'd been running her own business for years and it felt as though a piece of her was missing now that she no longer had the freedom to make her own decisions.

Charlotte eyed her thoughtfully. "You know, there's a large retail shop space opening up across from Whimsical Delights. Someone was going to rent it for an art gallery, but that fell through. I've given some thought to renting it for my own art gallery, but the space seemed too big. What if we shared it? You could have a portion for your interior design samples and an office space. Or maybe even sell some home décor items."

Gretchen stared at them. "You know, that's not a bad idea. You wouldn't believe how many of my real estate clients ask me about where to buy quality furnishings for their vacation rentals. A combination art and interior design business would be perfect. It would be like a one-stop shop for home decorating."

A rush of endorphins swirled around in Amelia's brain. She could picture it now – a thriving interior design business and a chance to make her mark on her new hometown.

It all came thudding down when she quickly remembered why it wouldn't work. Aidan needed her at the hotel, and she'd committed to being his partner there.

"It wouldn't hurt to look into it, right?" Maura asked. "You did such a wonderful job designing the hotel's interior."

"Maybe. I don't have a lot of free time though." She'd originally thought that once they'd opened the hotel, she'd have some time to take on a few interior design clients but running the hotel and the small jobs she was doing for Gretchen's husband, Parker, and his friend, Patrick, had maxed out her schedule. Maybe once they had a good support team in place at the hotel and the busy summer season was over, she could consider taking on another client. She couldn't fathom ever having enough time to run her own shop though.

The food arrived and they stopped talking for a few minutes as everyone dug into their lunches. Amelia practically inhaled about half of her salad, then came up for air. The other women did the same.

"That was delicious." Maggie glanced ruefully at her hamburger plate, which now held only a few fries and a dollop of ketchup. "I was starved."

"Me too." Maura picked up the last quarter of her chicken salad sandwich. "With school ending, I've been so busy that I haven't had a chance to go grocery shopping this week. All I have in my house is some brown bananas and a stale loaf of bread." She took a huge bite of the sandwich.

Amelia ran her fork through her salad, hoping to find some more glazed pecans – her favorite part. Should she bring Jordan here when she showed him around town later? Everyone seemed to like the food at Off the Vine, but she hadn't been in town long enough to get a good feel for everything Candle Beach and nearby Haven Shores had to offer.

She looked up at her friends. "If you guys had out-of-town visitors, where would you take them to dinner?"

"The Bluebonnet Café, of course." A huge smile spread across Maggie's face.

Gretchen rolled her eyes. "You have to say that." She

looked at Amelia. "The Bluebonnet Café is great, but if you want another option, I really like the Seaside Grille."

"Or Arturo's in Haven Shores," Charlotte said. "The food is wonderful, and I love their romantic lighting." She zeroed in on Amelia's face. "Ooh. Is this a date?"

Amelia's face warmed and she took a long drink of water. "Uh, not a date. There's a guest at the hotel and I promised I'd show him around town."

The other women exchanged glances.

"So you promised a male hotel guest that you'd go to dinner with him?" Gretchen laughed. "I'm pretty sure that would be considered a date."

"Totally." Charlotte leaned over the table. "Who is it? Is he nice? Cute?"

An image of Jordan's classic features and engaging grin flashed into Amelia's mind and she felt a smile slip over lips. "He seems nice." She sighed. "And yes, he's very attractive. But it's still not a date. I think he's just lonely."

"Uh-uh." Maggie shook her head knowingly. "Rule number one in the hospitality industry: the guests are not your friends. If this guy had wanted a restaurant recommendation, he would have asked for one. He wanted a date with you."

Amelia's stomach flip-flopped. She'd tried to avoid thinking of it as a date because things were already complicated with Jordan. For one thing, he thought she was a maid at the hotel, and for another, he'd be leaving town soon and going back home to California. There wasn't a future for them together, even if they'd both felt the same connection.

She waved her hand in front of her. "He's here by himself and he's lonely. I don't think he plans to propose to me anytime soon, okay? Don't get so excited." She eyed her friends. All of them were married or in serious relationships and they seemed to think she needed the same thing. "I'm not looking for romance. With the hotel opening, we're booked steadily for the summer and I don't have the time right now to pursue an interior design business, much less a relationship."

Amelia's friends stared at her, and she realized that her words had come out much harsher than she'd intended. She stared down at the remains of her salad.

Maura pressed her lips together, then opened her mouth and said in a quiet voice, "I don't think Aidan would want you to give up a chance for happiness, either with the design business or with this guy."

Amelia sighed. "The guest in question will go back home in a few days and I'm working with my brother in a business we own together. Believe me, I'm not giving up anything." To her own ears, her words sounded hollow, and she hoped the others wouldn't hear it too.

Charlotte leaned over and wrapped her arms around Amelia's shoulders, her touch quelling some of the pain that lurked just below the surface of Amelia's skin. Amelia allowed herself a moment of pity, then forced a smile. She'd chosen this life and would have to make the best of it.

6

Jordan stared at himself in the mirror. Was a button-down shirt too much? Should he have gone with a more casual polo? For the first time in a long time, he felt out of his element. This thing with Amelia – was it a date? Did she consider it as such? He didn't even know if he considered it a date. All he knew was he couldn't get her out of his mind, and he wanted to get to know her better.

He ran his hands through his hair and took one last look at his reflection. He wasn't ready for the big screen, but it would have to do. Now if only he could make the tension he'd glimpsed on his face disappear before he had to go downstairs and meet Amelia.

He grabbed his wallet and jacket and made his way down to the first floor. They'd arranged to meet on the front porch at five thirty and he was a few minutes early. He waited – and waited – on the porch. At a quarter to six, he was starting to wonder if he'd been stood up when Amelia came running up to him, out of breath.

"I'm so sorry. I was working on something and got lost in it." She smiled apologetically at him.

The tension left his body as soon as he saw her. Her face

was flushed from rushing around and her light brown hair was slightly tangled where it hit her shoulders. He'd never seen anyone look as beautiful wearing a simple sleeveless blouse and white capri pants.

Never? A sharp pain stabbed at his chest. He'd just admired another woman and hadn't even compared her to Annie. What exactly did that mean?

"Jordan? Are you okay?" Amelia asked.

He shook his head and smiled at her. "I'm fine. You look great." If he didn't stop being so neurotic, he didn't stand a chance of having her be interested in him.

She glanced down at her clothing and then back at him. "Thanks, I think. I didn't even have time to change after work."

Her words struck him as odd because when he'd first seen her, she'd been wearing a crisp turquoise maid's uniform. But maybe she'd been assigned to a different task for that day. Come to think of it, she didn't really talk about her work much.

"So, I was thinking I'd show you around town a little first and then we can grab a bite to eat. What type of food are you interested in? We've got the Bluebonnet Café, the Seaside Grille for seafood, Chinese food, and pizza in Candle Beach. Oh, and a wine bar that serves a wide variety of food. Or, if you want to see Haven Shores too, there's Arturo's for tapas and a great Thai place." She walked down the steps toward the parking lot, and he followed her. When they were next to a compact blue Toyota, she pulled out her keys and unlocked the car using the key fob. "I figured I would drive, if that's all right with you."

"Sounds good to me. That way I can see everything without worrying about running into something." He got into the passenger seat. Her car smelled good – a faint floral aroma – but he didn't see an air freshener. "The Bluebonnet Café. Is that where you get the morning pastries from?"

She nodded as she checked her mirror and began to back out of the parking spot. "Yep. My friend Maggie owns it. Everything there is excellent." The tires crunched on gravel as she drove out of the parking lot and onto the paved highway. Her gaze darted over to him. "Did you want to go there?"

"If the rest of their food is half as good as their pastries, I'll love it." He looked out the window as she drove down the highway. The stretch of road they were on was forested, but every so often the trees opened up to reveal a surprise view of the Pacific Ocean. At this time in the evening the sun was getting lower in the sky, but still provided ample daylight. He rolled down his window and let the breeze flow into the car. The scents of pine trees and saltwater mingled in the air. He turned to look at her. Her eyes were on the road as she piloted the vehicle around the sharp curves. "Where are we going first?"

"I'm going to take you to one of my favorite overlooks," she said. "It's right before you get to town – you probably passed it on the way in."

"I saw something, but I didn't want to stop. I got to the airport in L.A. so early yesterday morning that I was exhausted by the time I arrived in Candle Beach. All I wanted to do when I got to the hotel was to take a nap." He grinned, remembering checking into the hotel and meeting her for the first time. When she'd seen him at the desk with Aidan, her face had scrunched up into an adorable expression of horror. "Luckily, my room was clean and ready for me."

Her lips twitched and spread into a smile, but her cheeks had turned a charming shade of pink. He knew he should stop teasing her, but he loved watching her reaction.

She flicked on the turn signal and drove into a long parking lot on the beach side of the road. Here, no tall trees obstructed the view and he could take in the mighty expanse of ocean. They got out of the car and walked over to the edge of the overlook, which had a wooden railing as a safety barrier. Below them, a path wound its way down the incline.

She pointed in the distance. "That's the Peril Island lighthouse."

He turned in that direction. Far out to sea, a lighthouse perched on a rocky outcrop, flashing about every ten seconds. He looked at the island and then his eyes moved to the beach below them. Huge rocks stuck out of it, like pillars of sand rising to meet the sky.

"Wow. I wouldn't want to be sailing through this area back before they put in a lighthouse. I bet a lot of ships crashed on those rocks." He could easily imagine how perilous this coastline would be during one of the harsh winter storms Amelia had told him about.

"I know. It's crazy how things are so calm right now, but when it's dark and rainy, everything looks so different."

They were both quiet for a moment as they gazed at the lighthouse.

She lightly touched her fingers to his arm to get his attention, sending the hairs on his skin into high alert at the unexpected touch. She pointed further down the beach. "That's the Candle Beach marina over there and you can see parts of town too. I think that's why I like this overlook so much. When I first moved up here, I stopped at this spot, and it was my first impression of the town."

From this viewpoint, the town was charming. "I'm looking forward to seeing it," he said.

She eyed the sun. "We'd probably better get going if you want to see everything before dark."

When she spoke of her adopted hometown, her face lit up. He allowed his eyes to trace the curves of her face. "I'll be here for a few more days. We don't have to see everything today."

She froze for a second and his blood turned cold. Mentioning a future outing with her had been too much, too fast, hadn't it?

She recovered quickly. "I think we can see most of it today, but there might be something we miss."

He slowly let out the breath he didn't know he'd been holding. She wasn't too upset. "What's next on the agenda?"

"I was thinking we'd take a tour of town. We might need to save Bluebonnet Lake for another day."

"Bluebonnet Lake? Is that what the café is named after?" He'd never even looked at a map before coming to Candle Beach and now realized how little he knew about the area.

She laughed. "Yep. And the elementary school and a number of other things. Well, technically they're all named after the bluebonnets that grow near the lake."

He took one last look at the coastline and they got back into her car, heading north.

The road curved and a dark blue lake, its far side lined with trees, came into view. A yellow farmhouse and a barn were situated closer to the road.

"Is that Bluebonnet Lake?" he asked.

"Yes. Maggie, who owns the café, also owns the old farm property on the lake. She's turned it into an absolutely gorgeous space for events. We can see it in more detail another day."

"Okay. I'd like that." He watched as the lake and barn disappeared from view. A few minutes later, she slowed and turned off on a smaller street bordered by stores on one side and a grassy park on the other.

"And this is Candle Beach." She stopped at the only

stoplight he could see, giving him a chance to take it all in. "Isn't it cute?"

"It is." It was like something out of one of the small-town romantic comedies he'd been in. The Hallmark Channel would be all over a town like this. "I feel like we've gone back in time."

She laughed. "It does give that impression. Anyway, that's one of the town's bigger parks on our left. The Blue-bonnet Café is on the corner up there. I'll drive around town for a couple of minutes and then we'll come back and eat. Okay?"

He nodded. In his excitement about seeing Amelia again, he'd temporarily forgotten that he wasn't just a typical guy. He was a celebrity and when he went out in public, he was often mobbed by fans. He was wearing sunglasses, but he'd left his hat behind in his hotel room. There wasn't time to get it now though. With any luck, everyone would be like Amelia and not recognize him.

She drove through the town, pointing out the bookstore her friend owned and the local schools. Soon enough, they were parked in front of the Bluebonnet Café.

The glass window was so clear that he could see a baker's case filled with goodies and people milling around inside the restaurant's lobby. His stomach grumbled at the thought of the delicious pastry he'd had that morning. "I hope there isn't too long of a wait for dinner."

She laughed as she got out of the car. "Hungry?"

"Maybe just a little." He winked at her. They walked into the café together. When they accidentally bumped into each other as they went through the doorway, the now-familiar tingle ran through his body.

The hostess had just left the area to seat the couple who'd entered the restaurant as they were parking the car, leaving the two of them alone in the lobby. He walked over to the bakery case. They had pecan pie – his favorite.

"Picking out dessert already?" Amelia teased him.

"Hey, they might run out by the time we finish dinner. I've learned to always get my dessert with my meal. You never know what will happen." In his case, that was usually because the paparazzi had gotten too close, forcing him to grab his food and go.

A very pregnant woman came into the back corner of the lobby through a set of swinging doors. "Amelia!" She gave Amelia a big hug, then turned to him. Her eyes widened immediately, and his stomach sank. "You're Jordan Rivers, aren't you?" she whispered in awe.

He gave her a small smile and nodded, then glanced at Amelia, who was eying her friend with much confusion.

"Maggie, have you and Jordan met already?" She shot him a puzzled look.

Maggie stared at Amelia like she was insane. "Why didn't you tell me that your mystery man was Jordan Rivers?"

"Okay, what am I missing here?" Amelia's voice was thick with frustration. "Would someone please tell me what's going on?"

Maggie's eyes darted between the two of them as though they were a ping-pong ball in the last game of a match.

He sighed and faced Amelia. "Maggie knows me because she's seen me in a movie. At least I assume she's seen one of my movies or TV shows."

Maggie nodded. "I loved you in Tomorrow Someday." Her eyes took on a dreamy look. "Jake and I saw it a few months ago. It was so romantic."

Amelia's expression turned to one of betrayal. "Wait, so you're like a movie star or something?" She stared at him, as though begging him to deny it.

He felt the blood drain out of his face. "Yes. I've been in a few movies."

"Uh, I'm going to leave the two of you alone," Maggie said. "It sounds like you've got some things to talk about." She took a few steps backward, swiveled, and scurried back through the swinging doors.

"Yeah. I think we have some things to talk about." Amelia took a big breath, then grabbed his hand and led him over to a bench in the corner of the lobby.

He allowed her to take the lead as they sat on the bench together, their bodies turned to face each other, but their knees not quite touching. He scanned her face but couldn't figure out what she was thinking. Still, the fact that she hadn't run out of there when he'd confessed to omitting a pretty big detail about himself was encouraging.

"I'm really sorry I didn't say something before." He stared down at his hands and then back up at her. "When you didn't seem to recognize me the first time we met, I was surprised. And then we had such a nice time together on the beach. I didn't want to ruin it."

"Ruin it?" Her eyes scanned his face.

"Yeah. When people know who I am, they tend to only see me as Jordan Rivers the movie star, not Jordan Rivers, an ordinary, imperfect human being." He sighed loudly. "I get a lot of people who only want to be around me for my star power, not for who I am."

"Ouch. I can see why you didn't say anything." Her eyes danced. "Actually, as long as we're confessing things, I have a confession of my own."

His heart stopped. Was she going to tell him she was secretly married or something?

"I'm not really the hotel's maid. I co-own it with my brother, Aidan."

"Aidan's your brother?" His pulse returned to normal.

She nodded.

"But wait – why didn't you say something before? Why did you let me think you worked at the hotel as a maid?"

She shrugged and gave him a lopsided smile. "I acted like such an idiot when we first met that I didn't want you going on social media or something and lambasting the hotel for having such an unprofessional owner. When you assumed I was the maid, it was easier to let you think that."

He laughed. "I wouldn't have said anything. But I think we need to start over." He held out his hand to her. "I'm Jordan Rivers. Yes, Jordan the movie star."

A wide smile crept across her face. "And I'm Amelia, the co-owner of the Candle Beach Hotel." She reached out and shook his outstretched hand "Nice to meet you, Jordan."

The hostess approached them.

"Table for two?" She looked like she was fighting to contain her excitement over meeting him, but she held it together and didn't ask for his autograph.

He looked over at Amelia and she smiled at him. "Yes, table for two."

7

"Of course, Mrs. Rosen. I'll have two more bath towels brought up to your room. Have a nice morning." Amelia hung up the phone and placed a quick call to the housekeeping staff.

Dolly, the new maid, answered on the first ring. "Housekeeping," she said cheerfully.

"Good morning, Dolly. Room 124 would like two fresh bath towels this morning."

"I'll bring them right up." The phone clicked off.

"Ma'am," a man's voice said. He and his wife stood in front of the desk, dressed in casual clothing.

She smiled at them. "Hello. What can I do for you?"

"We're in Room 206, and we'd like to extend our stay for two more days if possible."

She nodded. "Sure, let's see what we can do." She tapped on the keyboard to get to the reservation system and looked up the man's room number, then frowned. "I'm sorry, we have another guest checking into that room today. I could move you to another room for tonight and tomorrow."

The woman frowned. "I don't want to move. We have everything unpacked in the drawers."

Amelia stared at the screen, trying to remember what Aidan had said about moving guests around. She knew the reservation system could be finicky and she didn't want to mess things up. "Hmm." It didn't look like the incoming guest was staying more than one night, so she moved him to another room, then moved that couple to yet another room. Finally, she had everything arranged. She looked up at them with a big smile. "Okay, I think everything is worked out now. I've got you down in Room 206 for two more nights."

"Excellent," the man said.

"Thank you so much." His wife beamed at her. "We just love the hotel and Candle Beach is so cute that we wanted to stay for a little longer."

"The town definitely grows on you," Amelia said. The couple walked out the door with smiles on their faces.

The phone rang and she answered it. While she was responding to the potential guest's questions about the hotel and their reservations policies, Jordan walked into the lobby.

Her stomach fluttered. He wore jogging pants, a t-shirt and huge sunglasses. She shot him a smile and he paused in front of the desk. The caller kept asking more and more questions, some of them repetitive. All Amelia wanted to do was get off of the phone and talk to Jordan, but she tried to keep the irritation out of her voice.

In front of her, Jordan shifted on his running shoe clad feet. A group of guests came in and stood in front of her as well. He looked nervously at the others in the lobby, then silently pointed at the door, to indicate he was heading out.

Her heart dropped, but she nodded that she understood. A minute later, the potential guest finally made a reservation for early September. As soon as she was off the phone, the people in front of her crowded in toward the desk, firing questions at her in rapid succession.

Where was Aidan? He was supposed to be up at the front with her to deal with the morning crowd.

She smiled at the guests and politely addressed their concerns. Thirty minutes and way too many guest interactions later, Aidan came into the lobby from outside, carrying a stack of long white boxes.

"Sorry, there was a mix-up with our morning pastry order from the café. I didn't want there to be a rebellion if we ran out of bear claws too early." He rushed into the Great Room with the boxes sliding precariously atop each other.

They must have reached the buffet table safely, because he returned in a minute, empty-handed. He peered at her. "Hey, are you okay?"

She nodded. "I'm fine. Just a little frazzled. I think half the guests wanted sightseeing information about the area or a change made to their reservation."

He stopped and stared at her. "You didn't change anything did you?"

She stared back him. "Only a few things."

"Ugh. Okay." He came around the other side of the desk and she slid off the stool in front of the computer to allow him to take over. "The reservation system's been acting up lately. I've got a call in to the company we bought it from, but I haven't heard back from them yet."

"I'm sorry. I didn't know," she said.

"I told you it had issues." He logged in with practiced movements.

"Yeah, but that's not the same as broken." She was really starting to hate working the front desk.

"I'm sure it'll be fine." He gave her a tight smile. "We received a letter from the state. They want us to call them about some kind of historical site listing. Can you please take care of it? I left it on the desk."

"Sure." She pushed open the door to the office, feeling as though she'd been dismissed by her teacher. Sometimes she felt more like an employee of the hotel than a co-owner.

She located the letter and called the state, then worked through a few more business matters. Around lunchtime, there was a knock on the door.

"Come in," she called out, still looking at the paperwork strewn out in front of her on the desk.

Elvis, the handyman, appeared in the doorway looking apologetic. "I'm sorry Amelia, but there was a problem with the flooring order for the cottage."

"What happened?" she asked. Even though she couldn't see it from the windowless office, she found herself turning in the direction of the caretaker's cottage.

"The planks the hardware store received for your hardwood floors aren't the right size. They're going to have to reorder the correct flooring."

"So, what does that mean? How long do you think it'll be until the floors are done?"

He fidgeted with the clipboard he held in his hands. "Another two weeks, most likely."

Her head buzzed. "Two weeks?" She'd counted on having the cottage done soon to give her a little space of her own

"I'm sorry, ma'am." He hung his head. "There isn't much I can do about it. I can try to push them to get the planks in faster, but I don't know if it'll work."

She sighed. "Keep me posted. Thanks for letting me know about the delay."

He nodded briskly and pivoted, hurrying away from her office.

She leaned her elbows on the desk and rested her head in her hands. By all accounts, the hotel was a roaring success, so why did she feel like such a failure? Every time she saw the hotel, she admired its beauty, but it felt like any other interior design project she'd finished for a client, not something of her own.

When her cell phone rang, she wanted to scream. Instead, she calmly removed it from the corner of the desk and checked to see who was calling.

"Hey, Charlotte," she said. "How's it going?"

"Good," Charlotte's cheery voice answered. "Actually, I'm calling to see if you wanted to grab lunch with me."

Amelia looked around the office. The walls of the small room seemed to close in around her. "I'd love to get out of here."

"Great! How do you feel about pizza at Pete's, in about twenty minutes?"

Amelia's mouth started to water at the image that popped into her head – a big, cheesy slice of Hawaiian pizza. "Pizza sounds amazing. See you then."

She hung up the phone, grabbed her jacket, and let Aidan know she was heading out to lunch. He was busy with guests, but he smiled and waved to let her know he'd heard.

Pete's Pizza hummed with activity as people ordered their pizzas by the slice or by the pie, plates clinked together in the kitchen, and the cash register clanged as it opened and closed. Charlotte and Amelia ordered their slices and drinks and sat down to eat at a table for two near the back of the restaurant.

"Wow, I've never been here for lunch before," Amelia said. "I can't believe it's so busy."

Charlotte smiled. "It's not like this during the winter, but during the summer months, everything in Candle Beach is slammed with tourists."

"Must be good for sales at your shop then." Amelia bit into her pizza, letting the saltiness of the Canadian bacon and mozzarella cheese blend on her tongue with the fresh burst of pineapple.

"It is. We've had to restrict the amount of people that can go into the Airstream trailer at one time," Charlotte said. "Otherwise, it would be crammed with customers shopping for gifts and no one would be able to move."

Amelia laughed, thinking of people stuffed like sardines into the old silver trailer that housed Charlotte's shop, Whimsical Delights.

"Speaking of tourists," Charlotte said as she put down her pizza. "I'm hearing rumors that Jordan Rivers is in town and you're dating him."

Amelia sputtered and almost choked on her pizza. Leave it to Charlotte to get right to the good stuff. She wiped her mouth with a paper napkin. "I'm not sure that we're 'dating', but we've hung out together a few times."

Charlotte's eyes sparkled as she leaned in. "Ooh. Tell me about him. Is he nice? I've always thought he looked like one of those actors who'd be nice in real life." She sighed. "He's so dreamy looking."

Amelia grinned. She was still trying to get used to the idea that Jordan was a celebrity. "He seems like a great guy. He has a little girl, and his wife died a few years ago, so he's a single dad."

Charlotte's eyes widened. "Oh wow. That's got to be tough. Is his daughter here with him?"

Amelia shook her head. "Nope. He came up here for a little vacation by himself." She suspected that Jordan had come to Candle Beach to figure some things out, but she didn't tell her friend that.

"And he found love with you." Charlotte beamed. "It's so romantic!"

"I don't know about love," Amelia said. "We just met a few days ago." She shrugged. "But I think things are going well between us." It was difficult to wrap her head around the thought that she was dating a man who was not only a single father, but a bona fide movie star. His life was so different from hers, but it made their connection even more fascinating.

"Are you going to introduce him to all of your friends?" Charlotte eyed her intently. "I'd love to meet him."

So, this was what it was like to date a celebrity.

"Um, he's only up here for a few more days, so I don't know about that." She had the feeling that Jordan would rather lay low while he was in Candle Beach and stay out of the spotlight.

"Oh." Charlotte pouted, then brightened. "Well maybe some other time."

"Maybe." Amelia sipped her drink. She had no idea where her relationship with Jordan was going, so she didn't want to make any promises she couldn't keep.

"Have you given any thought to my idea about opening up a combination art gallery and interior design business?"

Amelia finished chewing the bite of pizza that was already in her mouth and carefully set the rest of the slice on her plate. "I told you yesterday, it's not in the cards for me."

"Why not?" Charlotte asked. "I think you'd really enjoy it and I know it would be a big hit with the tourists."

"I don't have time for things like that," Amelia said. "We just opened the hotel and there's too much to do."

"But that won't always be the case, right?" Charlotte daintily wiped her mouth with a paper napkin emblazoned with the restaurant's name. "I would think things would calm down after a while."

"I don't know." She hadn't really thought much about the future at the hotel because every time she thought about things like arranging for more toilet paper or guest towels for the rest of her life, it made her ill. She loved the idea of her interior design business sharing space with an art gallery. Helping people find the right designs and objects to make their house a home was what she was passionate about. There was nothing better than seeing a client view their home in a completely new light when she was done with a project.

"Can you at least think about it a little? I'll need to know soon though, because I'm sure the space across from my shop will be leased quickly. It's a prime location for tourist traffic." Charlotte sipped her soda through a straw.

"I'll think about it, but I'm fairly certain it won't work." A heaviness settled in Amelia's chest and she wished she hadn't finished the last few bites of pizza.

"Okay. That's all I can ask for." Charlotte smiled at her, then checked her watch. "I'd better get back to let my assistant go to lunch too."

They stood from the table and the empty spots were immediately snatched up by a couple waiting nearby. At the corner of the street, they said goodbye and Charlotte walked down the hill toward her store, while Amelia got into her car and drove back to the hotel. As always, the sight of the ocean brought her joy, but seeing the hotel itself increased the weight on her chest.

When she walked back in, Aidan was the only person in the lobby. "How was lunch?" he asked.

"Delicious. They make the best Hawaiian pizza I've ever had." She leaned against the front desk. "This town constantly surprises me. Did you get lunch? I should have brought you something."

He shook his head. "Maura stopped by and brought me a sandwich to eat at the desk. I was too busy with some guest issues to leave the area." He took a deep breath. "I wanted to talk to you about the reservation you changed this morning."

Ice shot through her veins. "Okay."

"When you changed the first reservation, it had a ripple effect on all of our reservations for the day. When the guest you moved to allow that couple in room 206 to stay longer arrived, something had gone wrong with the system and the room he was assigned was double-booked." His delivery was flat, as though he were trying to stay calm.

"Oh no. I didn't mean for that to happen," she said.

"I know, but that's why I warned you not to move people around – at least not until I can get the system fixed." He swore under his breath. "I wish that company would call me back so we can get this situation resolved."

"I'm sorry," she said again.

"Just don't do it again. Okay?" This time, his tone bordered on condescension and she snapped.

"Look, I didn't mean to mess things up, but you left me alone at the desk and I didn't realize the system was that badly screwed up." She felt the stress of everything well up in her body – the cottage delay, Charlotte's art gallery offer, and how frustrated she was with working at the hotel. "I don't even want to be here. I hate everything about this."

His head snapped back, and he looked at her in horror. "What? What do you mean you hate this?" He examined her more closely. "I thought this was what you wanted."

Tears sprang from her eyes. "I thought I did too." She almost choked getting the words out, especially seeing the hurt on her brother's face. She glanced at the door. Free-dom. "I have to go."

She ran out the door, tears streaming from her face, and didn't stop until she'd run down the stairs to the beach and could feel a little peace. This wasn't how she'd pictured anything going. She'd never meant to hurt her brother, but her emotions had all bubbled up at once and spilled out without warning. Now how was she going to fix things with Aidan?

8

Jordan had just come down the stairs from his room when he heard Amelia and Aidan talking in the lobby. Although he couldn't make out what they were saying, Amelia's words were heated, and he paused at the foot of the stairs to avoid interrupting their conversation. When Amelia took off running, he immediately followed.

As he rushed past the front desk, he caught sight of Aidan's face. He looked shell-shocked. Whatever Amelia had said to him had taken him by surprise and he didn't say a word when Jordan passed by.

Outside, Jordan scanned the grounds and caught a glimpse of Amelia's hair flying behind her as she approached the top of the steps to the beach. He sprinted across the lawn and went down the stairs as fast as possible while still keeping her in sight. When he caught up with her, she was leaning against a log, her sides heaving as tears poured from her eyes.

"Amelia?" He moved closer to her. "Are you okay?"

She looked up and wiped away the tears, a futile gesture as they were quickly replaced by fresh ones. "I'm fine."

She was not fine. His pulse quickened as he stood there

with his arms at his sides, not knowing what he should do. If this were a romantic movie he was acting in, the script would usually call for him to take the woman in his arms and hold her, while kissing her passionately until she stopped crying. He wasn't sure Amelia would take too well to that. He settled for putting his hand on her arm and standing close to her to let her know he was there for her.

She collapsed into him, sobbing. He awkwardly wrapped his arms around her and held her tightly, letting her take the lead. After a few minutes, she pushed herself away and wiped her face on her sleeve, while looking in the direction of the hotel, high above them.

"I'm sorry. I got your shirt all wet." She tipped her chin at a large dark spot on his green polo shirt.

"Don't even worry about it." He scanned her face. "What happened? I heard you talking with Aidan, but I didn't catch what you were saying."

"Oh, it's nothing." She sniffled and sat on the log next to them.

He sat next to her, close enough that his arm touched hers. "It didn't seem like nothing."

She looked up at him. "I hate owning a hotel."

He pulled his head back and stared at her. "You hate the hotel? I thought it was your dream."

She sighed. "I thought so too. Turns out I only liked the *idea* of owning a hotel. While we were in the design phase, I loved it. It's the biggest interior design project I've ever worked on and I loved every minute of it – researching the hotel's past, finding exactly the right furniture for all of the rooms, everything. But now that we're actively operating it, I'm finding that I really don't like managing the place."

"Does Aidan enjoy it?" He reached over and moved a lock of her hair out of her eyes.

She laughed. "He loves it. He's always worked in the hotel

69

industry and now he finally has a chance to make a property his own. And he's really good at it." A tear slipped out of her eye. "But I'm not. I don't like dealing with angry guests or hiring new housekeeping staff or anything. Pretty much the only thing I like about it is having the opportunity to live in a space I designed – I've never experienced that before."

"And you told Aidan all of this just now?"

"Kind of. I pretty much blew up at him over a mistake that I made. I didn't mean for it to come out like that. In fact, I didn't mean for it to come out at all."

"You weren't going to tell him?" he asked.

She gazed out at the ocean. "I don't think I told you the whole story before, but our parents were killed in a car accident a few years ago. That's how Aidan and I had enough money to invest in the hotel – from their life insurance policies and by selling their house in the Bay Area."

"I'm sorry. That must have been a rough time for you." He swallowed a lump in his throat thinking about Annie's death. She'd been ill for a while before she died, and they'd been able to make the most of their time together. He couldn't imagine what it would be like to have two important people in his life ripped away from him without warning.

"It was." She was quiet again for a moment. "But we got used to life without them and I knew Aidan had always dreamed of owning his own hotel. When a friend alerted him that the Candle Beach Hotel property was on the market, he was instantly enamored with it." She laughed. "You should have seen the place a few months ago. Everything about it was falling apart. We worked miracles to get it ready in time for the summer tourist season."

"Aidan wanted to use your inheritance to buy the hotel?"

She nodded. "Yeah. And don't get me wrong, it wasn't

like I didn't want to buy it. The idea of fixing up the place intrigued me, and I was fully supportive of using our joint inheritance to purchase it. I guess it's just that I didn't know what I was getting myself into. I've always been really independent in my career and having to answer to someone else has taken some getting used to."

"But now you don't want to be a hotel owner," he said slowly.

"Right. A friend of mine, the one who painted all of those gorgeous paintings in the hotel's hallways, suggested that we open a combination art gallery and home furnishings store together. I'd have an office there too for my interior design business."

"That sounds perfect."

"It would be, except I already have a job – helping to manage the hotel." She frowned and kicked the side of the log she was sitting on. "I made a commitment to Aidan, and I need to see it through."

"But surely he'd understand."

"Probably, but I don't want to put him in that position." She turned to face him. "Have you always enjoyed being an actor?"

He shook his head. "Yes and no. There have been times where I wished I hadn't taken on a particular role, and the hours are horrible for a single parent." A sadness came over him. He wished he had spent more time with Annie instead of taking a role while she was sick, and the long hours weren't making it easy to be a good parent to Mia. Still though… "But I love taking on a character that had previously only existed on paper and bringing it to life. Knowing that people are entertained by my acting has always brought me joy."

"That's how I feel about my design career," she said. "I

love seeing how happy people are when they enter a room we envisioned together."

"You should go for it. Tell Aidan you want to make a change."

She jumped off of the log. "Maybe. I'll think about it." She turned back to him and reached out her hand. "C'mon. I want to show you something."

He wrapped his fingers around her palm and walked beside her for about ten minutes, feeling the warmth of the sun on his face and the intoxicating feeling of being close to Amelia. When they reached a large creek, she led him alongside of it until the sand ended and the water wound its way through a wooded area.

She pointed up the slope that rose above the stream. "This is one of my favorite places in the area."

They climbed the moderate incline until they arrived at an established trail. All around them, old-growth forest towered high over the trail and creek below. Moss dripped from the tree branches and thick burrs protruded from many of the trees. A soft covering of pine needles and moss cushioned the ground beneath their feet. The trail crossed under the highway, following the creek into the forest. When they were further inland, she stopped at an old, roughly-hewn bench by the side of the trail. Years of initials and hearts had been carved into it and it rocked slightly as they sat down on it.

"Listen," she said.

They sat there together, listening to the forest. It was both eerily quiet and bursting with life at the same time. Birds chirped from nearby tree branches and the creek bubbled through rocks and fallen branches in front of them. But there was a silence on the trail that he'd never experienced before. He immersed himself in it and let his thoughts wander.

Being with Amelia was like a salve to his soul. On the way to this spot, he'd thought briefly about Annie, but his thoughts now weren't consumed by how much he missed her. He looked over at Amelia. Her eyes were closed and relaxed, her long natural eyelashes kissing her skin. She was mesmerizing.

As if she sensed him staring at her, her eyes popped open. He turned away quickly, but it was too late.

"You were supposed to be listening, not looking at me," she teased.

His lips twisted into a grin. "I couldn't help it. You looked so cute sitting there, communing with nature."

She mock glared at him and pushed herself up from the bench. He stood too and put an arm around her waist, pulling her around to face him. He heard a sharp intake of breath as her eyes searched his face. He bent down and kissed her lips. They were as soft as he'd imagined. She snaked her arms around his neck and stood on her tiptoes to kiss him more deeply. He felt whole with her, just like he had with Annie.

He broke their embrace, then swore under his breath.

She stared up at him, hurt swirling in her eyes. "Did I do something wrong?"

He certainly wasn't going to tell her that he'd been thinking about his dead wife while he was kissing her. What had he been thinking anyway? He'd loved sharing the kiss with Amelia, so why did he feel like he was cheating on Annie? He walked away from her a few steps, knowing that he was hurting her, but not knowing what to say.

Her footsteps sounded on the trail behind him. She tapped him on the shoulder. "Are you okay?"

He looked into her face and his heart melted. "Yeah. I think I am." He reached for her hand and squeezed it. "I'm sorry. You're the first woman I've kissed since my wife died."

"Oh." She moved in front of him, her hand still in his. "Is this okay? If you're not ready to date, I understand."

He took a deep breath. She was being more than understanding, but he had to let go of the past. "No, I'm ready. Amelia, I really like you and I want to see where this thing between us can go."

She smiled up at him and her eyes locked with his. "Me too."

He wrapped his arm around her waist, and they turned around on the trail, heading back toward the hotel. Their topics of conversation on the way back were lighter in nature, but with every word they said to each other, he felt more connected. The instant spark he'd experienced with her was exactly the same as it had been when he'd met Annie, but his relationship with Amelia was different, maybe because they were older and had lived through so much more than two kids who were just starting college. Whatever it was, he wanted more of it.

9

"Did you talk to Aidan yet about starting your interior design business back up again?" Maura asked as she removed four dinner plates from an upper cabinet in her kitchen.

Amelia shook her head. "Not really. I apologized for blowing up at him, but then a guest issue came up and we didn't finish our conversation. I think he's trying to forget that it ever happened, and I'd like to do the same." Her stomach clenched and she had to remind herself that it was her decision to put her dreams aside to help Aidan with his.

"You have to tell him." Maura set silverware on top of the plates, then brought all of them into the dining room and placed them on the table. "The hotel is important to him, but *you* are more important to him than it is."

"I feel the same way about him, which is why I'm not going to say anything." Amelia sighed and picked up the four glasses Maura had left on the counter. "Can you please not push it anymore?"

"Okay, but I don't think Aidan has forgotten about it." Maura peeked in the oven. "Looks like the chicken is almost done. What time do you think Aidan and Jordan will be here?"

"They said they'd leave the hotel around six, so it should be soon."

"I still can't believe you're dating Jordan Rivers." Maura sighed dramatically. "Half the women I know would kill to date him."

Amelia shrugged. "He's just like any other guy – well, a nice one I mean. He's not stuck up or anything like that."

"I wouldn't think so if you were interested in him," Maura said. "Carrie always said he was a nice guy though. I only met her sister a few times, but I was sad to hear of her passing. That's got to be hard on him, losing his wife and being left alone with a young daughter."

"Yeah." Other than mentioning her a few times, Jordan didn't talk much about his wife. "Maura, what was Annie like?"

"Hmm..." Maura sat in a kitchen chair. "She was really sweet, outgoing, and just generally nice. She and Carrie were pretty close, but she and Jordan had already moved to L.A. by the time I went to school with Carrie, so I didn't know her too well."

Maura's corgi, Barker, sounded an alert to notify them of the threat of intruders, followed closely by the more orderly ringing of the doorbell.

"Ah, sounds like they're here." Maura popped out of her chair and strode across the small living room to the front door. She opened it wide to allow Aidan and Jordan to enter, giving Aidan a kiss on the mouth as he entered. Jordan crossed the room to Amelia and stood close to her, almost as if she was his security blanket.

"Hi, I'm Maura," Maura said to Jordan with an outstretched hand.

He flashed her a confident smile, suddenly every inch the movie star. "Nice to meet you, Maura. I'm Jordan."

Amelia was used to seeing Jordan when it was just the two of them, so it was interesting to see how his persona changed when he met new people who recognized him.

"I'm so happy you were able to come here for dinner," Maura gushed. Amelia smothered a laugh. She hadn't expected her calm and collected friend to be so starstruck upon meeting a celebrity.

"Hey, what about me?" Aidan asked. "Aren't you happy I'm here for dinner too?"

Maura laughed. "Of course I am, but I see you every day. Jordan is our guest of honor." The timer binged on the oven. "Speaking of which, I think our dinner is done." She gestured to the dining room. "Why don't the three of you have a seat and I'll bring everything in."

"Do you need help with anything?" Jordan asked.

"Uh, yeah, do you need help?" Aidan asked.

Amelia just grinned and walked into the kitchen, where she grabbed the dinner rolls she'd seen Maura put in a cloth-covered basket and brought them into the dining room.

"Sure, I'm happy to put you to work. The sooner we get the food in there, the sooner we can eat." Maura led them into the kitchen and handed each of the men a serving dish filled with food. Soon, they were all seated around the table and ready to eat.

"It's been a while since I had a home-cooked meal." Jordan dug into his mashed potatoes that he'd covered with brown gravy. "I'm usually home too late to eat with anyone."

"It must be difficult to be away from home so much," Maura said. "Do you ever have to work on location?"

He nodded. "Unfortunately, yes. I hate being away from

my daughter, Mia, for so long, but luckily my sister-in-law Carrie is there to help. You know Carrie, right?"

"Yep, we go back a long time." Maura beamed at him. "When she called me to ask if there was room for you to stay at the hotel, I had the worst time not telling everyone in town that you were coming here."

Jordan grinned. "Well, thank you for not spreading the word. It was nice to have a few days up here before people started to recognize me. Thank goodness I managed to charm Amelia before she realized that I was a no-good actor." He nudged Amelia with his elbow.

"The jury's still out on that one," she said dryly.

"Amelia, be nice!" Aidan said, trying hard not to laugh.

"Oh, okay, I kind of like him." She turned to Jordan and he leaned closer to kiss her cheek.

"Well, that's a relief." He pointed to his food. "Maura, this chicken is excellent."

She turned beet red. "Thank you. I got the recipe online, but I wasn't sure if you were used to fancier food."

"Nope. I like pretty much anything." He buttered and ate a piece of a dinner roll, as if to make a point.

Amelia watched his exchange with Maura. Thank goodness he was getting along with her friend. When Maura had proposed dinner at her house, Amelia wasn't sure it was a good idea, but Maura had convinced her to try it out. It was nice to go out together though, and for Aidan to get to know Jordan a little better. In a short amount of time, Jordan had quickly become an important part of her life and she hoped her brother would like him too.

"So, you'll only be in town for a few more days?" Maura asked. "Do you have plans to come back up here again, or will you be filming a new movie soon?"

Amelia eyed Jordan. They hadn't talked too much about plans for the future. Most of their time together had been spent getting to know each other while experiencing everything the town and local area had to offer. She knew he'd only be in town until the end of the week and she hadn't wanted to think about where things would go after that.

"I'm definitely planning on coming back up here, although I'm not sure yet when that will be. I need to talk to my agent and figure out my schedule. Plus, I promised my daughter I'd take her to Disneyland next week. She'll be out of school for the summer and we haven't taken a family vacation in years." He looked over at Amelia. "I was hoping Amelia might be able to come and visit me soon though."

Amelia's face grew heated. He hadn't mentioned her visiting before. "I'd love to. That is if Aidan can spare me from the hotel."

Aidan looked at her. "That's probably something we should talk about, among other things. But someone has been avoiding me for a few days." He cleared his throat and narrowed his eyes at her.

Amelia squirmed in her seat. She didn't want to have this conversation with Aidan –

not now or ever – even though everyone seemed to think they knew what was best for her.

Maura slugged him lightly on the shoulder. "That's probably something you can discuss some other time. Not at dinner."

He nodded. "I agree. Not right now." He eyed Jordan. "You must have traveled to some amazing places. Care to tell us about any of them?"

Jordan laughed. "You mean like the cornfield we filmed in while we were in Illinois? Or the cow pasture in Vermont?"

"Seriously?" Amelia asked. "What kind of movies were these?" She cast a glance at her brother to see if he still seemed upset with her, but he had a huge smile on his face.

Jordan laughed again. "Small-town romantic comedies. I get typecast as the boy next door who the leading lady eventually realizes is her one true love."

"Ah. I love those types of movies." Maura sighed. "They always have a happy ending."

"Yep. And I do love playing in them, but sometimes I wish I had the opportunity for some more serious roles." He helped himself to more mashed potatoes.

"Well, I'll have to watch some of your movies after you leave. Now that I know the leading man, I may be more interested in watching something made in this century." Amelia laughed as she took a bite of chicken.

"Don't go falling for any of my characters though," Jordan said. "I'm not nearly as nice or handsome as they are." He reached under the table for her hand.

Amelia smiled up at him and she squeezed his hand, her heart warm and full. "I don't know about that. I think you're pretty great."

"Okay, okay. Enough gushiness already." Aidan turned to Maura. "Were we this sappy together a few months ago?"

"Probably." She looked over at Amelia and Jordan, then gave Aidan a kiss. "But I'm still pretty fond of you."

"The feeling's mutual." He gave her a loving glance.

"Uh, I think you're still pretty sappy together." Amelia was glad though that her brother had found someone as great as Maura to both challenge and support him.

"I have a German chocolate cake from the bakery, but I'm really full right now." Maura eyed her plate. "Does anyone want to play a board game or something before we have dessert?"

"Sounds good to me." Amelia helped Maura to clear the table while the others picked out a game for the four of them to play.

In the kitchen, Maura said quietly, "I think Jordan is great. You picked a good one."

Amelia peeked into the living room to check on their progress. "I know. I really hope it works out between us. I don't know how the long-distance thing will work, especially with him having a daughter. I haven't even met her yet." She laughed nervously under her breath. "Then again, when you think about it, I've only known him a few days. But still... I really like him, and I think we have a good chance for a future together."

"Don't stress about it too much," Maura said. "Things have a tendency to work out."

"I hope so." Amelia wasn't usually the type to worry, preferring to cross bridges when she came to them, but Jordan was a movie star and probably had women throwing themselves at him all the time. Would the relationship they'd developed in their whirlwind romance be enough to counteract that?

With the last dinner dish stowed in the dishwasher, Amelia put a smile on her face and walked out to the living room. She and Jordan may only have a few more days to spend together before he had to go back to his regular life in Los Angeles, and she intended to make the most of every one of them.

10

Jordan woke the next morning to gray skies and a heavy fog that seemed to intensify the roar of the ocean, bringing it straight into his room through the open window. The morning light irritated his eyes and he rolled over in bed to face the wall, pulling a pillow over his head. He and Amelia had been out late the night before, trying out a new restaurant in Haven Shores, followed by a long walk on the beach together. Their nightly walks had become a highlight of his stay in Candle Beach that he would sorely miss when he had to return to L.A. the next day.

His phone vibrated on the nightstand, but he ignored it. Anyone who was calling him at six-thirty in the morning could wait. It stopped, but then began its vibration cycle again. He was tempted to throw it across the room but picked it up instead.

Vincent. Why was his agent calling him so early in the morning? He checked his voicemail. Three messages from Vincent. He'd known he'd missed some calls, but he hadn't realized it was that many. The cell phone service in Candle Beach could sometimes be spotty, so they must have come in when he wasn't in a good area for cell phone reception. He hit play and Vincent's booming voice came over the phone's speakers.

"Jordan. You're not answering – again." Vincent sighed dramatically. "I need to talk to you about a new role that just came up. A big name canceled on the studio and now they want you to audition for the part. This could be your big break."

Jordan stared at the phone. He was considered successful in the film industry, but he wasn't at the top of the A-list actors. Vincent was usually a straight shooter. If he thought this could be the role of a lifetime, he meant it.

Jordan listened to the rest of the message.

"I'm flying up to Seattle this morning to see you. I should be in Candle Beach around..." There was a silence on the phone and Jordan imagined Vincent was checking the driving distances. "...one o'clock. I'm planning on meeting you for a lunch." A flight announcement interrupted him, and he finished the call.

Great. Vincent was coming to Candle Beach. As much as he liked his agent, the idea of someone from his life in L.A. coming to town made him feel a little ill. Other than seeing Mia, he would be happy to stay in Candle Beach forever.

His eyes had adjusted to the light, but the glare from the gray skies still bothered him, so he shut the curtains, cloaking the room in darkness. He felt his way over to the table lamp and flicked it on. A soft glow filled the room, providing enough light for him to find his workout clothes. His daily run had become an important part of his routine in Candle Beach, and as the time neared to return home, he hoped it was a habit that would stick.

He and Amelia had plans for dinner that night, but she was working until five o'clock. It wasn't that he didn't have time to meet with his agent. He just didn't want to deal with anything regarding his life back home while he was still in the safe embrace of Candle Beach.

He jogged down the steps and out the door. He'd heard about the heavy fog on the coast but hadn't yet experienced it. Most of the mornings he'd been there had been beautiful and clear, so today he was seeing everything in a new light.

He jogged over to the stairs to the beach but detoured to the beautiful wooden gazebo nearby. He'd seen it before but hadn't gone inside. Slowing his steps as he neared the structure, he took it in. A thick mist swirled around the posts and the octagonal roof, giving it a spooky appearance that would make any horror-movie director proud.

He stepped inside. In sharp contrast to the exterior, the inside was cheery. Someone, perhaps Amelia, had placed throw pillows in a red-and-green flowered outdoor fabric on the freshly painted benches. The result was a warm, inviting atmosphere, much like Amelia's own personality.

He took a look through the telescope mounted on a railing, but he could barely see the water below in all the haze, much less a whale. The benches were inviting, and he wanted nothing more than to curl up on them and take a nap. He forced himself out of the gazebo and down to the beach, stretching lightly before he broke into a jog that took him down to the waterline.

When he returned to the hotel an hour later, breakfast had been set out in the Great Room. He grabbed a pastry, waved at Aidan and went up to his room to shower. After his shower, the light on his phone was blinking to notify him of a text message from Vincent.

"Just landed in Seattle. See you around one."

The message filled him with dread, and he felt like a little kid balking at a visit to the dentist. He eyed the scripts that Vincent had sent him over the last few days. Better to get it over with before his agent got there.

He immersed himself in the scripts. Some were horrible, but others pleasantly surprised him. One in particular caught his attention – a family drama. As much as he appreciated the industry's continued support of his acting talent, he was tired of being pigeonholed into roles as the lead in a romantic comedy. He flagged the script he liked, then moved on to the next one, but it stayed with him and he found himself subconsciously comparing all of the others to it.

At twelve thirty, Vincent called from the road to set up a place to meet.

"Hey Jordan, you finally answered."

"Yeah, sorry about that. Cell phone reception isn't always great here." Might as well blame all of it on the cell service, rather than tell his agent he'd been blatantly ignoring him.

"Uh-huh." Vincent's tone left little doubt that he knew Jordan had been blowing him off. "Anyway. Good we connected now. I should be there in thirty minutes. You've been there almost a week – what's a good place to eat? I imagine I can't expect much."

Jordan chuckled. He'd thought the same of the small town on the Washington coast. "You'd be surprised. Let's do the Bluebonnet Café. You'll see it on your way through town. It's on Main Street and you can't miss it."

"Sounds good." Vincent paused. "I'm really glad to have a chance to chat with you. It's been a while, buddy."

"It has," Jordan agreed. "I'll see you soon." After hanging up the phone, he stood and stretched. Vincent was the closest thing to a friend that he had, and Jordan trusted him – something that wasn't common in the industry. He pushed away the doubts about his L.A. life intruding on his cozy nest in Candle Beach and headed out the door. He'd be a little early to the café, but that meant he'd have plenty of time to select his dessert ahead of time.

Jordan had already chosen two pastries as an after-lunch dessert by the time Vincent arrived for their meeting. The staff at the café didn't seem as starstruck anymore – probably because they'd been warned about his presence by Maggie – so after he purchased his treats, he was able to sit in the lobby wearing his sunglasses and hat without being disturbed too much.

Vincent entered the building, flipping his sunglasses up before scanning the lobby. A wide smile crossed his face when he saw Jordan. Vincent came over to Jordan and clapped him on the back.

"Hey, man. You look fantastic. Are you staying at a spa or something?" He looked around. "What smells so good in here?"

Jordan just grinned and pointed at the bakery case. He knew Amelia was the reason his stress lines had disappeared, and his spirits had lifted. Vincent moved over to the bakery case and his eyes lit up as much as Jordan's had when he first saw the display.

"I'm definitely getting that boysenberry pie after lunch," Vincent said. "I'll have to work it off at the gym, but I hope it'll be worth it."

Jordan laughed. "It will be, but you're going to want to buy it now or it may not be there after lunch." He motioned for the woman behind the counter to box up a piece of the pie, then paid for it.

"Hey, I'm supposed to be buying you lunch." Vincent took the box from him. "But thanks."

"Are you ready to be seated?" The woman who'd rang them up asked.

"We are. Thank you." Jordan flashed her a smile and she blushed.

"Right this way, gentlemen." She led them over to a table in a private corner of the restaurant.

"Is any of the food here edible?" Vincent asked as he perused the menu.

"Everything here is really good. I told you. Candle Beach is full of surprises." Jordan made his selection and put his menu down on the table. "What did you want to talk to me about that couldn't wait? I'll be back home tomorrow."

Vincent took a final look at the menu, then set it down on top of Jordan's menu. "You'll never believe this, but Andrew Fider dropped out of the new Kingston movie – and they want *you* to audition for the part."

Jordan's jaw hinged open. "You're serious?"

"Uh-huh." Vincent beamed. "They want you. But if you're not interested, I'm sure they have a long list of other actors who'll want the part."

"Oh, man." Jordan sat back in his chair. This role was a dream come true. Adair Kingston was known for his action movies, a far cry from the romantic comedies he'd always acted in.

"What can I get for you two?" a forty-something waitress with curly brown hair asked. "Would you like something to drink to start?"

"I'm going to have an iced tea and the club sandwich," Jordan said.

"Iced tea and the chicken Caesar salad please. Dressing on the side." Vincent patted his stomach. "Got to watch the calories if I'm having that pie for dessert."

The waitress smiled and nodded. "Dressing on the side. Got it." She pivoted and strode off toward the kitchen.

"What do you think about the role?" Vincent asked. "It's a great opportunity, right?"

"It is." Jordan was quiet. "But when does it start filming? And where will they film it?"

"That's the best part: it starts next week and they're aiming for an eight-week filming schedule," Vincent said.

The waitress came by and he took his drink from her, immediately taking a huge gulp of it. "Airline travel always makes me so thirsty."

"The location?" Jordan prompted.

"Oh yeah. It's filming partly in L.A. You won't even need to leave the area. Well, except for maybe a few weeks that they'll shoot up in Vancouver."

"Vancouver?" Jordan wasn't sure he wanted to be gone from Mia that long. And what about Amelia? How was he going to maintain a long-distance relationship with her if he was working the crazy hours that went along with filming? Worry clouded his thoughts.

"It won't be too bad – only a few weeks and you'll be home. You still have your sister-in-law around to watch your daughter, right?"

"Yeah." He knew Carrie would be happy to help out with Mia and managing the household a little longer, but she needed to move on with her life. She'd already given up too much to help them.

"What's your hesitation?" Vincent asked. The waitress placed a giant bowl of salad in front of him and his eyes grew as big as saucers. "This is huge!"

The waitress smiled at them and set a club sandwich with fries in front of Jordan, along with a bottle of ketchup. "Is there anything else I can get you?"

Jordan and Vincent exchanged glances.

"Nope, I think we're good here." Jordan eyed her name tag. "Thank you, Nancy."

She turned as red as the ketchup when he said her name. "Um, enjoy." She scurried away to the far side of the restaurant.

"Even though I've been in this business for a long time, I still can't get used to how people react when they meet one of my clients." Vincent shook his head.

"I know." Jordan dipped a fry in ketchup. "It gets a little annoying. I always feel like I have to be someone I'm not when I'm in public."

"Hey, I'm just glad you're a decent guy." Vincent drizzled Caesar dressing over his salad. "I never have to worry about you. Some of my clients have my PR team on speed dial."

"I try," Jordan said. He'd never understood why some stars thought they had a license to act badly in public, just because they were household names and made obscene amounts of money.

"So, the gig?" Vincent asked. "Are you in?"

"I don't know." Jordan inhaled deeply, then let it out slowly. "When do I need to let you know?"

"In the next few days, at the very latest." Vincent stared at Jordan. "Why would you not be interested? Is there something I don't know about?"

His mind flashed to Amelia's smile when she said goodbye to him the night before. Being with her had felt like home – something he hadn't had since Annie died.

"I've met someone up here." He looked down at his plate. "That type of role would be all-encompassing. I'd barely have time to sleep for the next two months and there definitely wouldn't be any extra time to spend with her or Mia."

Vincent whistled under his breath. "She must be pretty special."

"She is." Was he really doing this? Thinking about giving up the role of a lifetime to spend more time with Amelia and his daughter? Happiness flooded over him as he envisioned the two most important females in his life meeting each other. Yes, it would be worth it. Still though...it was the role of a lifetime.

"I'm surprised the tabloids haven't caught wind of your mystery woman yet," Vincent said.

Jordan's stomach twisted. He'd been so caught up in his feelings about Amelia that he hadn't given much thought to how the media would treat her. Would she be able to handle the spotlight? Or would it be too much for their fledgling relationship? He'd have to broach the subject at dinner that night.

"I haven't seen anything yet. We've kept it fairly low-key in the area." Jordan shrugged. "Then again, I haven't been keeping up with the news either while I've been here. For all I know, the media's already planning our wedding."

Vincent's eyes darted around the restaurant. "Quiet down, or you'll be married off before you expect it."

A vision of Amelia in a white wedding dress, standing at the altar, floated into Jordan's mind and took him by surprise. What was more surprising was how right it felt to think of himself being the man who'd join her in front of all of their family and friends. He shook his head to clear the image. What was he thinking? They'd just met less than a week ago and hadn't even discussed their future.

"Sorry," he said. "I guess I've been lulled into a false sense of security here in Candle Beach. Things are so different here than they are back home. It would be a great place to raise a family." The words popped out of his mouth before he'd thought them through.

Vincent peered at him. "You're not thinking of moving up here permanently, are you?"

He hadn't been, but what was holding him back? He and Annie had always been frugal, and he'd banked most of what he'd made over the years in his film career. There was plenty for a nice house in Candle Beach where Mia could make lifelong friends that weren't spoiled rotten by their uber-wealthy parents. And Amelia lived in Candle Beach...

He shrugged. "I don't know. Maybe?"

Vincent's eyes closed for a moment and he sighed. "I'm losing you, aren't I?"

Jordan laughed. "I wouldn't say that. All I'm saying is I think it might be the right time to make some big changes in my life. Whether those will be with my career, my residence, or a mental shift only, I don't know yet."

"Fine. But I expect to hear from you about this role within a few days. And I'll be bummed if you don't take it." He shot Jordan an imploring look. "If you turn this role down, you probably won't be offered anything similar ever again."

Jordan pressed his lips together. "I know. But it's a chance I'm willing to take." He finished off his sandwich and pushed the empty plate to the side. "Now, how about we have our desserts and table this conversation for a few days."

Vincent smiled and reached for the box containing his pie. "I can live with that."

11

Amelia stared out the window of the hotel's owner's suite. Normally, she'd be looking at the caretaker's cottage and dreaming about having her own space, but today, she was too preoccupied.

This was it. The last time she'd see Jordan while he was still in Candle Beach. Would it be the last time she'd ever see him? Her stomach churned and pain shot through her chest at the thought of never seeing him again. So far, they'd avoided talking about the future, but tonight was now or never for that discussion.

Someone knocked on the door, startling her from her thoughts. She ran her hands over the skirt of her sundress to smooth a few wrinkles, took a deep breath and opened the door.

"Hey." She looked up at Jordan and their eyes met.

"Hey yourself." He gave her a quick peck on the cheek, then eyed her dress. "You look gorgeous."

"Thank you." She smiled up at him. Her mood felt as floaty as the flowered skirt that swirled around her legs. She'd bought it back in San Francisco but had never found the right occasion to wear it before today. It seemed like the perfect thing to wear to the picnic she'd planned for the two of them.

He moved out of the way as she stepped into the hallway, closing and locking the door behind her. They'd already had a few guests try to enter their private quarters, thinking it was an access to the guest wing.

"Where are we going?" he asked. "You said you were planning something special."

"I am." She gave him a secretive smile. This was fun. "C'mon." She grabbed his hand and they exited the building through the lobby, then walked around the side of the hotel until they reached the little cottage. "But first, I wanted to show you the progress on my cottage."

"Ah-ha. So, this is the famous cottage you've been telling me about. I can't believe it's taken so long for you to take me here."

She laughed as she unlocked the door. "I didn't want to show it to you earlier because I was hoping the floors would be done by the time you left." The door swung open and she pointed at the plywood subfloors. "Obviously, they're not."

"It's a cute place. I can see the potential." He walked across the living room and peered out the back window. "You've got a nice view from here."

"I know." Every time she was in the cottage, she loved it more and more. This was the place that she was going to make her own and would make Candle Beach feel like home. "Elvis already has the walls painted and all the plumbing and electric has been updated. So, once the hardwood floors arrive and are installed, I'll be able to start decorating and moving in."

"That's exciting." He went into the kitchen. "It's like something out of a magazine."

"Hey, I am an interior designer." Her stomach clenched. Well, not really anymore.

She showed him the small bathroom and bedroom, then they went back out to the living room. "I'm going to have my friend Charlotte paint me a picture of the hotel with the ocean in the background and hang it up over the fireplace. I'll have a nice long couch under the window for taking naps on, and a coffee table, and more art." The excitement rushed through her like electricity.

"Take a breath in there." He stood behind her and kissed the top of her head, sending more endorphins running through her. "I think it will be beautiful when it's complete. I can't wait to see it."

She turned to him, so close that their bodies were almost touching, and lifted her eyes to meet his. "Do you think you will see it?"

A puzzled expression twisted his facial features. "What do you mean?"

She took a deep breath. This was the now or never, and she'd never been one for tiptoeing into anything. "Are you planning on coming back to Candle Beach after you leave?"

He stepped back. "Of course I am. Why wouldn't I?"

"I don't know." She shrugged. "You're going back home and soon you'll be back in your real life – work, your daughter, parties. I don't know. Real life."

He laughed. "Yeah, not so many parties. I *am* looking forward to seeing Mia though. I miss her." He stared into space for a moment, as if envisioning his daughter.

Amelia should have been sad that he was so eager to go home, but she loved how much he cared about his daughter, even if he didn't think he was the world's best father. Her parents had been a big part of her life and it made her happy to see the love he had for Mia.

"I'm sure she'll be happy to see you too." She kissed him on impulse. "Wait a minute." She darted into the bedroom and removed a large picnic basket that she'd hidden in the closet.

"A picnic?" A slow smile spread across his face. "I love it."

"I thought we could picnic on the lawn out behind the cottage and then take a walk on the beach," she said. "That way, we avoid anyone who'd want to take their picture with you, and we can have a little privacy."

"I like the way you think." He reached for the handle and she gladly let him carry the heavy basket outside.

On the way out the door, she grabbed a thick blanket that she'd stashed in the living room. About ten feet from the cottage, she gestured to the grass. "Here is good." She flopped the blanket onto the ground and pulled on the corners to straighten it out. He set the basket on the blanket and she opened it up, revealing ham sandwiches, chocolate chip cookies, potato chips, cut fruit, and a pitcher of iced tea. "I'm not much of a cook, so I had Maggie put something together for us."

"No complaints here. Did she think you needed enough for an army?" He removed the plates that had been under the food and handed one to her, then filled his up completely with food.

"Ha-ha." She took a sandwich and some fruit, then poured iced tea into two wide-bottom glasses and set one in front of him on the blanket. Maggie had been so excited about her having a picnic with Jordan that she'd gone a little overboard.

He munched away happily on his sandwich, then devoured a cookie. She nibbled at her food but wasn't really hungry. This was their last meal together in Candle Beach and they still didn't have any definite plans to see each other again.

"What do you think you'll do when you get home?" she asked. "Are you starting a new movie?"

He swallowed the bite of cookie he'd been chewing. "I'm not sure yet. My agent was in town today and he presented me with a role that would be huge for my career."

"But?" she said. "It sounds like you have some reservations about taking it."

"I do." He used a fork to add some cubed cantaloupe and watermelon to his plate. "It would mean two months of pretty intensive filming, including a few weeks out of town."

"Isn't that normal though?" She ate a chip and followed it with a long swig of iced tea.

"It is, but I don't know if it's something I want to continue doing. It would mean long hours away from Mia... and I wouldn't be able to come up here to visit you." He scanned her face. "I'm not sure any amount of money is worth that for me at this time."

She stared at him. He was considering turning down the role of a lifetime – for her? "That's a lot to give up. Are you sure you'd want to do that?" She busied herself with straightening up some of the picnic items on the blanket, while sneaking a peek at him to see his reaction.

"I'm still trying to figure things out. Do you think you'd be interested in coming down to Los Angeles and staying for a week or so? I have to warn you though – things can get a little crazy with the paparazzi back home." He sighed. "The media attention is just an unfortunate part of my job."

She grinned. "I'd love to come visit you. And I'm not going to be scared off by some overzealous photographer." Then her heart sank, remembering that she was now the owner of a hotel in the middle of a very busy tourist season.

"But I don't think I can get away from the hotel until September. I don't want to leave my brother in the lurch."

"So, if I take the movie job, we won't see each other for a few months." He sighed. "Amelia, I don't want to go that long without seeing you."

"Me either." If this was what being in love with someone was like, she wasn't sure she liked it. Everything had become so complicated.

"You know what? Let's stop thinking about all of this right now." He stood and reached for her hand to help her up. "I think we should pack up the picnic stuff and head down to the beach now. I'm going to miss our nightly beach walks."

"Me too." Tears sprang into her eyes as they packed the food away and folded up the blanket.

They left all of the picnic supplies in the cottage and walked toward the beach holding hands. When they neared the gazebo, he stopped.

"Want to check for whales? I heard from another guest that they saw some humpback whales out there yesterday."

"Sure." She'd never had the good fortune to spot any, but maybe she'd been looking at the wrong time.

They climbed up into the gazebo and walked over to the telescope Aidan had installed.

Jordan peered through it first, then handed it over to her. She scanned the ocean, but all she saw were foamy tips on the waves. Then, as she was about to give up, she saw a tail flip up in the air as a whale dove down into the sea.

"I see one!" She pulled him toward the telescope. "Right there."

He looked in the direction she'd pointed out. "I think I see one too." He stepped back from the telescope. "It's so beautiful here. Back home, it's often so smoggy you can't see thirty feet ahead of you. Being in Candle Beach is like stepping back in time."

She nodded. "I've thought the same thing."

He put his arm around her waist and pulled her to his chest. "We're going to make this work."

"Okay," she whispered. Her brain was buzzing at his closeness and every nerve in her body shivered with expectation.

He tipped her chin up and kissed her, sending waves of happiness through her. She leaned against his chest, looping her arms around the back of his neck, and ran her fingers through his hair. His scent was an intoxicating blend of aftershave and "eau de chocolate chip cookie". He moved his hands down her back, settling just above her waist. They stood like that, locked together for what seemed like hours, but in reality, was more like minutes.

The sounds of another couple out for an evening stroll came near and they parted reluctantly.

"Time for our beach walk?" he asked.

She nodded, unable to speak. They made their way down the beach stairs and across the loose sand to right above where the surf crashed upon the shoreline. The tide was on its way out every step they took left footprints in the spongy, water-logged ground. Above them, the sun had sunk to just above the horizon, flooding the sky with purples, reds and pinks.

"This place is like something out of a movie," Jordan said. "I know several directors that would kill to film a sunset like that."

She squeezed his hand. "We have to have something to bring you back to Candle Beach."

"Uh, the sunsets are nice and all, but that's not what will bring me back here." He spun her around to face him and kissed her so deeply that the world started to tilt.

When he released her, she clung to his arm, not wanting to let go of him – or this perfect moment. She scanned his facial features, then closed her eyes, trying to memorize every detail she could. Whatever memories she could take in would have to last her a long time.

Every drop of sunlight had left the sky when he gently caressed her face and said softly, "We'd better head back to the hotel. I have to leave for Seattle at the crack of dawn tomorrow."

"I know." She wished that time could stand still, and they could stay in the moment forever, but she knew he needed to get some sleep before driving his rental car to the airport.

They walked in silence back to the hotel, then stopped in the deserted lobby.

"I don't want to make this any harder than it already is," he said. "I'm going to kiss you goodbye and then head up to my room, okay?"

She nodded. It was tearing her apart to have him leave and prolonging the goodbye would only make it worse.

He reached for her and pulled her close into a tight embrace. She wrapped her arms around him, feeling his warmth mix with hers and the strong connection between them. He kissed the top of her head and she looked up at him. Tears streamed down her face as their lips met.

He closed his eyes, then opened them and stepped back. "I'll see you soon."

"See you." She watched as he turned away from her and walked slowly into the hallway leading to the guest rooms. When he'd disappeared from sight, she brushed the tears away from her cheeks as much as possible before approaching the owner's suite.

With her hand on the door handle, she paused. She didn't want to enter the apartment she shared with Aidan yet, so she went back outside and into the cottage. She refolded the blanket into a semblance of a seat and sat down on the floor, letting her emotions flood over her. Would she see Jordan again? And if not, would her life ever be the same?

12

It had been four days since Jordan left Candle Beach and Amelia missed him more than she'd expected. It felt like she'd lost a part of herself when he left, and it seemed like her worst fears were coming true – now that he was back home, he didn't have time for her. She'd tried calling a few times, although she hadn't left a message. He'd sent her a few quick texts in return to let her know he was thinking of her but was swamped at work. However, he had said he'd call her tonight, so she was going to take that as a positive sign.

She finished getting the breakfast area set up in the Great Room, arranging the pastries and coffee urns in a neat line as the guests hovered around her like wolves, ready to pounce. Her phone rang in her pants pocket and a thrill shot through her. Jordan!

She reached for the phone, but it was only Gretchen.

"Hey, what's up?" she asked.

Gretchen's voice bubbled over the phone, each word catching on the next in her excitement. "Maggie had her baby last night!"

"Oh, wow." Amelia moved aside to let the wolves get to

the pastries and walked outside to get more privacy. "How's she doing? How's the baby?"

"They're both doing well," Gretchen said. "She and Jake haven't decided on a name yet though."

"Still?"

Gretchen laughed. "He's got some strong opinions against most of the names she's picked out. If I know Maggie though, she'll wear him down soon."

"Is she still in the hospital?" Amelia asked. "Can I come visit her and the baby?"

"She's in the hospital in Haven Shores and asked me to let everyone know they're welcome to visit, as long as they're up to date on all of their immunizations and will promise to wash their hands."

"Ooh, I'm so excited," Amelia said. "I love new babies."

"I got a chance to see her this morning," Gretchen said. "I'm not a huge baby person, but I have to admit, she's a cutie. Maggie's in the maternity ward, room 418."

"Well, tell Maggie I'll be there around lunchtime. I can't wait." She said goodbye to Gretchen and hung up the phone, silently assessing her workload for the day. She wasn't scheduled for desk duty, so it shouldn't be too difficult to get away for a couple of hours.

She worked until noon and then drove to the hospital in Haven Shores. At five stories, it was one of the tallest buildings in the area. Even though she'd never been inside, it had caught her eye the first time she'd seen the town.

As she rode the elevator up to the fourth floor, she wondered how it would change things in her group of friends with Maggie and Dahlia both having babies. Maggie was the only one of her new friends who already had a child, but Alex was at the age where he was already in school and didn't need as much supervision all the time. Amelia had only been friends with Maggie and Dahlia for a few months, but from what she'd heard, babies took up every ounce of available time.

She knocked on the door to room 418 and Maggie's husband, Jake, came to the door.

"Hi, Amelia. Maggie will be happy to see you. Some of the other girls were here earlier, but they've already left. She's having a good time ruling the roost from her bed." He grinned at his wife, then turned back to Amelia. "Actually, would you mind staying with her? I'd love to run down to the cafeteria. They brought food for Maggie, but I'm on my own and I didn't want to leave her alone." He gave Maggie a look that was so full of love that it shot daggers of jealousy into Amelia's own heart.

"Sure, I'm looking forward to seeing the baby." She and Jake exchanged places and she entered the room.

Maggie was propped up on the narrow hospital bed with three pillows behind her. Her baby girl was lying on her chest, wearing only a diaper and a loosely wrapped swaddling blanket. Maggie's hands dwarfed the baby as she gently wrapped them around her back to make sure she wouldn't slide off.

"Hi," Maggie said. "Don't mind if I don't get up. She just fell asleep." She grinned wryly. "Plus, I'm still a little shaky on my legs."

"I didn't expect you to get up." Amelia smiled at her. "Maggie, she's beautiful."

"I know," Maggie whispered as she stroked a wisp of hair that curled out over the baby's ear. "She's so tiny and perfect. It's hard to believe Alex was ever this small. They grow so fast." A tear slipped out of her eyes and she grabbed a Kleenex from her side table to wipe it away.

"Don't cry." Amelia came over to her bed. "Are you okay?"

Maggie chuckled. "Yeah. I have so many hormones

rushing around that any time I think of something remotely sad, the waterworks start. I'm fine." The baby opened her eyes for a second and then closed them again. "How are you doing? Is that movie star of yours still in town?"

"Nope. He went back to Los Angeles a few days ago." Amelia pulled a chair over to Maggie's bedside. "I haven't heard much from him, but he's supposed to call me tonight."

"Oh, I'm sorry, sweetie." Maggie laid her hand on Amelia's shoulder. "I'm sure he's just busy."

"Probably." Amelia's stomach swam. Maybe she was sick and shouldn't be around a newborn baby. She took a deep breath and the worry-induced nausea subsided. She'd never been in a relationship before that had made her feel like this – the high every time she thought about or spoke to Jordan, and low when she didn't hear from him. "It'll be fine though. Long-distance relationships are hard, but if it's meant to be, it'll all work out." Her mother had said that often and it seemed appropriate for this situation.

"You seemed happy with him though," Maggie said. "When you came into the café together, your face was glowing. You really like him."

"I do." Amelia looked out the window. Maggie's room had a lovely view of the ocean, which reminded her of all the times she'd spent on the beach with Jordan. "Actually, I think I may be in love with him." She gulped in a huge breath of hospital air at the admission.

"I knew it! I told Charlotte that things were serious between the two of you." Maggie grinned. "She didn't believe me."

"I guess they are – for me at least." Amelia stood and stretched her legs. "But I don't know if he feels the same way."

"I think you should go for it." The baby stirred on her

chest and Maggie shifted a little on the mound of pillows. "When you find love, grab hold of it and don't let go. After Brian died, I never thought I'd find love again, but Jake changed my mind. And now look at us – we have a beautiful little girl together."

As if hearing her mother talking about her, the baby's eyes opened, and she gazed at Maggie with curiosity.

"Do you want to hold her?" Maggie asked. "I need to feed her soon, but if you wash your hands, you can hold her first."

"I'd love to." Amelia rushed over to the sink and thoroughly washed her hands. She dried them off with a paper towel, then walked back to Maggie.

Maggie lifted the baby toward Amelia, who gently took her from her mother, supporting the tiny girl's head and neck with her right hand as she nestled her into the crook of her arm. The baby stared up at her, making Amelia's heart skip a beat. She'd often had doubts that she'd make a good mother but looking down into the eyes of this sweet little newborn, she knew it was something she wanted in her life. Was Jordan the man she'd spend the rest of her life and raise children with? She hoped so.

The baby girl started to pucker her lips in the air and Amelia handed her back to Maggie. "I think she's hungry." As if by magic, the baby nestled onto Maggie's chest. "She's adorable, Maggie."

"I know." Maggie's eyes filled with tears again. "I can't believe how happy I am."

"How does Alex like his baby sister?" Amelia asked.

"He was up here earlier today and he's in love with her as much as Jake and I are. I think he's going to be a great big brother." Maggie yawned. "They gave me the option to stay tonight in the hospital and I took it because it's nice to have someone cook and clean for me for once, but I wish they wouldn't wake me up every few hours to check vitals. I'm looking forward to being home tomorrow with baby girl. I know she'll wake me up to eat, but it's not the same as having some nurse come in and take my temperature."

"Do you want me to go so you can get some rest?" Amelia asked.

"I'll probably nap when Jake gets back. Until then, tell me about the hotel – have you had any interesting guests?"

Amelia rolled her yes. "Oh my gosh, yes. We've had some weird ones already. The hotel business is a never-ending source of entertainment." She launched into a story about a few of their hotel guests and Maggie's eyelids began to flutter. Jake came back in the room and moved the baby to her plexiglass crib next to the bed, then Maggie's eyes shut completely.

"She needed that sleep," Jake said. "She's been up all morning. Thanks for staying until I got back." He sipped his latte. "It's been a long night for both of us." He eyed the couch under the window longingly. "In fact, I might catch some shut-eye now myself."

"I'll leave you to it." Amelia took one last look at the baby, then let herself out of the room, gently latching the door behind her.

Would she ever be as happy as Maggie was with Jake? Everything between them seemed so easy that it was hard to imagine there ever being rough patches in their relationship. Maggie swore there had been some snags when they first got together, but they seemed to have worked through everything now. Amelia couldn't imagine a more perfect couple.

She took a deep breath. She'd learned long ago that you had to work for things that you wanted in your life. Her relationship with Jordan was no different. When she was in the parking lot, she called him. It rang a few times, and then a woman answered.

"Hello? Jordan's phone," the woman said.

"Uh…" Why was a woman answering Jordan's cell phone? "Is Jordan there?"

"I'm sorry, he's not available at the moment. Can I take a message?"

Amelia's head buzzed and she couldn't answer. Was this woman why Jordan hadn't been calling her?

"Hello?" the woman asked.

Amelia panicked and clicked the off button, then stared at the blank screen.

When she'd done a quick search on the Internet, she'd seen that Jordan had been linked with many women over the years. He'd told her about the constant paparazzi attention back home, and although he claimed the romantic entanglements were fabricated by the media, how much of it had been true? He was a movie star and women probably threw themselves at him. How easy would that be to resist? Had she been wrong about him?

With tears streaming down her face, she drove back to the hotel and locked herself in the caretaker's cottage. The flooring had arrived early, soon after Jordan left, and the handyman had installed it. She'd been moving things in, little by little, and now she collapsed onto a soft, microfiber couch she'd purchased for the living area. In the last hour, she'd gone from utter joy at the thought of having children with Jordan to worrying that he had quickly moved on to another woman. If this was love, she wasn't sure it was worth it.

13

Jordan hung up the phone and swore under his breath. He'd been calling Amelia for three days and had left her several voicemails, but she wasn't answering or returning his calls. What was going on?

When he'd returned home, he'd been slammed with things to do on the home front – end-of-year activities for Mia's class at school, a broken water heater at the house, and he'd given in to Vincent's request and auditioned for the role in the Kingston movie. He wasn't sure what he'd do if they offered him the role, but he figured it made sense to audition first and see how things went. It gave him a little more time to decide where he wanted things to go in his life. However, all of that had meant that he hadn't been able to do more than text Amelia for the first few days he'd been home. Had she taken that for a lack of interest on his part?

"What's wrong?" Carrie asked as she came into the living room.

"Amelia isn't returning my calls. I don't know what's wrong." Pain gnawed at his chest. He didn't want to lose Amelia. In the space of the week he'd been in Candle Beach, she'd become an important part of his life. Why had he let things at home take priority over communicating with her?

The color drained out of Carrie's face. "Uh, Jordan. I forgot to tell you something."

"What?" He peered at her. "Did something happen?"

"I think she may have called a few days ago. A woman called while you were in the shower. I didn't recognize the phone number, but I knew you were waiting for a callback about that audition, so I answered. She asked for you and I said you weren't available. I thought it was just some random woman who'd gotten your phone number because I assumed you'd have her name programmed into your phone. And then we went to Mia's end-of-year party and I forgot. If that was her, I'm so sorry."

"I didn't get around to adding her name to my address book when I was up there. Her number was always in my recent calls, so I didn't need it." He stared at the floor. Amelia had called and talked to Carrie. What had she thought when she reached a woman instead of him? "Did she seem upset when you answered?"

Carrie met his gaze. "Maybe a little surprised?"

"I'm concerned she may have received the wrong idea when you answered. You know how the paparazzi likes to make up stories about my love life."

"Oh no." She bit her lip. "Should I call her and explain? I feel really bad."

He sighed. "No. It's not your fault. I understand why you didn't say anything to her. I should have put her name in my phone." It was frustrating that Carrie had answered his phone and forgotten to tell him he'd had a call, but he couldn't blame her. The day of Mia's end-of-year party had been hectic, and she'd had a lot on her mind.

"What are you going to do? Do you think she'll answer you if you text her?"

He'd been in enough romantic comedies to know what he should do. "I don't know. I think I'm going to have to go back up there to Candle Beach and talk to her in person. I don't want any more miscommunications." He looked at Carrie. "Do you think Mia would want to come with me?"

She shrugged. "I don't know. Maybe? She's really excited about your trip to Disneyland this week though."

"Disneyland will be there in a week." They'd already made the reservations and they'd lose some money if they canceled, but that was the benefit of being rich – losing money didn't matter when more important things came up.

"I don't know that she'll see it the same way," Carrie said. "But I'm up for a trip to Candle Beach – that is if you want me to come with you. I can help watch Mia so you can spend some time with Amelia, and I'd love to see Maura again."

"Really? You'd do that for me?" he asked.

She laughed. "Of course. You may not believe this, but I want you to be happy and I think this woman is good for you. Besides, I'm sick of seeing you pine over her."

He grinned. "Thanks, Carrie. I'll give Amelia's brother Aidan a call and explain the situation to him. Hopefully he can squeeze us in at the hotel." Even if they couldn't get rooms at the hotel, Jordan would find some other place for them to stay. He had to see Amelia.

"I'll give Maura a call." Carrie pulled her phone out of her sweatshirt pocket and walked into another room.

Jordan dialed the number for the hotel's reservation line. He wasn't sure what he'd do if Amelia answered, but luckily, Aidan was manning the phone lines.

"Candle Beach Hotel, how may I help you?" Aidan asked in a professional voice.

"Hey, Aidan. It's Jordan." He paused. Had Amelia said anything to her brother about Carrie answering the phone?

Aidan's voice chilled a little. "Hi. Did you forget something here?"

"I was actually hoping that you might have some rooms available for tomorrow night. I'd like to stay for about a week." He sighed. "Look, I don't know what Amelia told you, but she's not returning my calls or texts. I just found out she called here a few days ago and spoke to my sister-in-law, who takes care of my daughter. I'm worried she may have thought it was a date of mine or something."

"Maura's friend Carrie?" A sigh of relief came over the phone. "I knew it had to be something like that," Aidan said. "I found her sitting on the floor of her cottage, bawling her eyes out. She told me what happened, but she hasn't mentioned it since. That's kind of how Amelia deals with things. She lets herself be upset for a day and then bottles up any other emotions to be slowly processed." He sighed again. "Not the healthiest method."

"I was afraid of that." Jordan stared at his phone. He had to get Amelia back.

"Okay. You're in luck. We just had someone cancel a reservation for tomorrow. I can fit you in for five days in one of our rooms with two queen beds."

"Only one room is available?" Jordan asked.

"Yeah. Did you need more?"

"My sister-in-law wanted to come up and visit Maura. I'll go ahead and take the room and figure out something else for her."

"Did you get a room?" Carrie asked from behind him.

"Hold on," he said to Aidan. He muted the phone and turned to Carrie. "Yeah, but they only have one room. If you still want to come, I'm sure I can find you somewhere really nice to stay. I'd really like to stay at the hotel though, so I'm closer to Amelia."

She grinned. "No worries. Maura just invited me to stay

with her. It'll be like old times in our dorm room. Maybe we'll even stay up all night talking about boys." She chuckled. "I'm looking forward to meeting her boyfriend, Aidan. If he's half as nice as she says, he's a keeper."

"I'll let him know that. I've got him on the line here." He pointed at his phone.

She blushed. "No! You can't tell him I said that." She looked at him in horror, making him laugh.

"Don't worry, I won't." He didn't have any sisters, but he'd always thought of Carrie as his little sister and loved torturing her like any older brother would. He unmuted the phone. "Hey Aidan, you still there?"

"I'm here," Aidan said. "Do you want me to put you down for the room?"

"Yep. Carrie's going to stay with Maura."

"Oh, great. Maura will love that." Aidan clicked away at a keyboard. "Okay, I've got you down for tomorrow night, staying for five nights."

"Thank you." A thought occurred to him. "Is Amelia going to be around tomorrow night?"

"She should be," he said.

"I wanted to surprise her when I get there. Will she be at the front desk?"

"I'll make sure she is," Aidan said. "I can't wait to see her face when you arrive."

"Well, I hope it'll be a pleasant surprise." So many things could go wrong with his plan.

"She doesn't seem too mad at this point, just a little sad. I think once you explain, she'll come around."

"I hope so. Thanks, Aidan." He hung up the phone and swiveled around to Carrie. "Okay, we're on for tomorrow night. I'll call the airlines and reserve our flights to Seattle and a rental car."

"I'll call the hotel at Disneyland," she said. "You know,

Mia won't be too happy about this, but I think you're doing the right thing."

"Thanks, Carrie." He impulsively gave her a hug. "I couldn't have asked for a better little sister than you."

She blushed again. "Annie would want you to be happy."

"I know." He stared at the picture of Annie and baby Mia that hung on the wall. "She told me she wanted me to remarry when I met the right woman. I just never expected it to happen so fast."

"When you know, you know." Carrie pointed at his phone. "Now book our flights! I'm going to call the hotel in Anaheim and get packing for me and Mia. We've got a lot to do before tomorrow."

He saluted. "Yes, ma'am." She left the room and a goofy grin came over his face. He'd see Amelia again tomorrow and he was going to win her back, no matter what it took.

14

"I like the bigger tile for the kitchen floors." Amelia tapped a sample tile with her index finger, then looked up at Parker and Patrick. "But I like those small blue and green ones for the backsplash in the kitchen. I think we can use them in the shower and behind the sink in the bathroom too, to keep the first-floor design consistent."

"I like it," Patrick said.

Parker picked up a tile and examined it more closely. "Me too."

"Great." She flashed them a grin. "I think this house is going to be gorgeous once you're finished with it."

"It'll be a hundred times better now that you're helping with the interior design," Patrick said. "I can refinish a handrail to perfection, but my design skills are limited."

"I agree." Parker jotted something down on the yellow legal pad in front of him. "This house is going to appeal to a wide range of buyers when we're done with it." He pushed his chair away from the kitchen table. "I knew Gretchen was onto something when she hired you to help us out with our new business."

"Yeah," Patrick said. "You should really hang up your

shingle here in town. As much as I'd love to keep your talents for us alone, we're only going to be able to do a few houses a year. There are plenty of people with summer homes that need decorators and have money to burn."

"Oh, I don't know." She smiled, but her heart ached a little. She still hadn't talked to Aidan about taking on design clients other than them. Things were crazy at the hotel, and with things up in the air with Jordan, it hadn't seemed like the right time. "I'm pretty happy with things right now."

"Okay, but let Gretchen or me know if you change your mind." Parker snapped his fingers. "I can probably round up a few new clients for you, just like that."

"Well, thank you. I'll think about it." She stood. "Speaking of Gretchen, I'm supposed to meet her for lunch today. I'd better get going."

"I'll call you next week to go over the plans for the upstairs," Patrick said. "I definitely want to get your opinion on the color schemes for the three bedrooms up there."

"Sure. Sounds good. See you later." She let herself out the front door of the old Victorian house they were reno-vating and got into her car. Before she drove away, she allowed herself a few minutes to let her emotions out in the open.

After calling Jordan and reaching some woman, she'd thought the worst of him. But he'd kept calling, and now she wasn't sure what to think. Had she been wrong about him? He'd never given her reason to doubt him before and she knew he'd had problems with the media blowing female attention out of proportion in the past. Maybe this was a big misunderstanding too.

She took a deep breath. She missed him so much that it hurt. She'd give herself another day to calm down about it and then call him back.

She drove away from the house and parked in front of

the Seaside Grille, where she was meeting Gretchen for lunch. When she arrived, she found Gretchen was already there, sitting at a large table near the long row of windows facing the ocean.

She sat in the chair across from Gretchen and set her purse on the floor. "This seems a little big for the two of us."

"Oh, I invited a couple more people," Gretchen said.

"Oh, okay. Some of the girls?" Amelia asked as she perused the menu. The crab melt sandwich sounded amazing, but she'd heard the lobster bisque was excellent too.

"Uh-huh." Gretchen waved at someone behind Amelia and she turned to see who'd arrived. Maura and Charlotte were making their way over to the table.

"Hi, guys," Amelia said. "I didn't know you were coming to lunch today too."

"Gretchen called me this morning and asked if I was free." Maura shrugged. "I don't have much to do in the summers besides my shifts at the Candle Beach Historical Museum, so I jumped at the chance to hang out with you guys."

"Me too." Charlotte sat down next to Gretchen. "Plus, I wanted to see if you'd given any more consideration to my idea for a combination art gallery and design business."

Amelia didn't answer right away. When were they going to give up on this? She'd told them over and over that she wasn't interested in pursuing a full-time interior design business in Candle Beach. With her duties at the hotel, there simply wasn't time. But she didn't want to upset her new friends either.

She smiled at Charlotte. "I don't think that's in the cards for me right now."

The waitress came over to the table. "Are you ready to order? Is everyone in your party here now?"

Gretchen exchanged glances with Charlotte and Maura. "We're still waiting on one person."

Amelia narrowed her eyes at Gretchen. Something felt off with this lunch. "Who are we waiting for?"

"Me." Aidan sat down across from Maura. He turned to the waitress, who was standing there, tapping her pen on her pad of paper. "I'm pretty quick at choosing. Can you get their orders first? I should be ready by the time you're done."

She nodded and looked at Amelia expectantly.

"Uh. The crab melt...and a cup of bisque." At this point, she didn't have the mental capacity to make a decision between the two menu items she'd been thinking about ordering. What was going on here?

The waitress moved on to Maura and the other women to get their orders.

"What are you doing here?" Amelia hissed at Aidan. "Who's watching the front desk?" She glanced at her watch. One o'clock. They couldn't leave the front desk alone in the middle of the day.

"Tania." He went back to his menu.

Tania? Who was Tania?

The waitress took Aidan's order and left them alone to stare awkwardly at each other.

"Okay. What is going on? Why is Aidan here?" She stared pointedly at her brother.

"We wanted to chat with you about your role at the hotel." He gave a look that was full of innocence.

"What do you mean?" she asked. Was this some sort of intervention?

"I'm hearing through the grapevine that you're not very happy working full-time at the hotel."

"I never said that." She picked up her glass of ice water and drained half of it in one long gulp.

He sighed. "But you did. You flat-out told me that you hated working there."

She laughed nervously. "I already apologized for that. I was a little overemotional that day. I didn't mean what I said."

He eyed her and said with an even tone, "I think you did."

She looked down at her napkin and then at her friends, who were sitting there quietly, taking it all in. "I may not enjoy working at the hotel as much as you do, but I made a commitment to you and I intend to honor it."

He reached across the table and covered her hand with his. "I don't want you to feel like you have to honor some commitment you made to me before you even experienced what hotel ownership was like." He sighed again. "Look, I love the hotel and I know you do too, but you don't love running it. That's fine." He glanced at the other women. "Charlotte tells me that there's an opportunity for you to open your own interior design business here in Candle Beach. I think you should go for it."

She peered at him, afraid to even dream that she could reopen her design business in a new location. "I can't do that. Who'll help you with the hotel?"

He grinned like a cat who'd caught a canary. "Ah. That's where Tania comes in. She's a friend of Maggie's and has experience in the hotel industry in Seattle. I've hired her to work full-time at the hotel and have been training her in secret for the last few days."

"What?" His words came slamming down on her. "You mean I no longer have a job at the hotel?"

"Nope." He smirked. "You're fired."

She stared at him, her thoughts suddenly filled with a mixture of fear and excitement. "But..."

"No buts. You need to go find yourself another job." His tone softened. "Of course, you'll always have a place at the hotel if you want it, but I think your talents would be better used elsewhere. From now on, you can consider yourself a silent partner in the hotel." He peered at her. "Does that sound okay?"

Okay? Her head buzzed. It sounded more than okay. She was free to do whatever she wanted. She took a long slow breath.

"Yeah. I'm good with that." A thought occurred to her. "I can still live in the cottage though, right?" Being jobless and homeless at the same time was not a pleasant combination.

"Of course. You still own half of the hotel, you just don't have to be involved with the daily operations." Aidan leaned back to allow the waitress to set his food in front of him.

"Okay." She idly stirred the bisque in front of her, watching the steam rise as the spoon moved between chunks of lobster.

"So now are you interested in my proposition?" Charlotte asked, eying her eagerly.

"Yeah." A warmth spread through Amelia's body. "I think I am."

"Yay!" Charlotte clapped her hands.

Maura leaned over and gave Aidan a quick hug. "Good job," she whispered to him. He turned and kissed the top of her head before digging into his salmon.

Gretchen's eyes danced. "You still have to work with Patrick and Parker on their renovation projects though. They need it."

Amelia grinned at her. "I know they do. They'll be my first official clients." Was this really happening? A whole new life was opening up for her in Candle Beach. Now if only she could work things out with Jordan, life would be truly perfect. There was no reason to put it off any longer – she'd call him tonight.

"I'll call the landlord and set up a tour of the retail and office space across from my shop," Charlotte said. "Last time I talked to him, he said he'd had a lot of interest in the space, but I made him promise to wait another week before he made any decisions about who to let it to."

"Thanks, Charlotte." Amelia lifted a spoonful of bisque to her lips and let the creamy, savory broth spill into her mouth.

The five of them enjoyed their meal together, talking animatedly about Amelia and Charlotte's future business and how the hotel was doing. By the time they'd finished, it was almost three.

As they stood to leave, Aidan said, "Oh, I forgot. You're not officially fired until tomorrow. I still need you to work your shift at the front desk this evening. Tania has something she has to do later today, and Maura and I have plans." He wrapped an arm around Maura's waist.

Amelia laughed. "I'll gladly work my last shift at the hotel." She sobered. "And Aidan?"

"Yeah?"

"Thank you." She stood on her tiptoes and kissed his cheek.

"No problem, sis. I can't even tell you how much I owe you for helping to support my dream of owning the hotel. I literally couldn't have done any of this without you. I should be the one doing the thanking."

Tears of joy beaded in the corners of her eyes. "I'm so happy that it's all worked out so well. Mom and Dad would be proud of what we've accomplished here."

He blinked back tears of his own. "I know." He released Maura for a minute and gave Amelia a huge hug. He and Maura left the restaurant together and the rest of them chatted outside for a few minutes before splitting off and going their own ways.

Amelia drove back to the hotel, ready to meet Tania and work her last official shift at the front desk. As soon as it was over, she planned to call Jordan and start her new life there in Candle Beach.

15

After a slightly bumpy flight, Jordan, Carrie and Mia arrived in Seattle early in the afternoon. Jordan had booked a rental car from the same agency he'd used before, and he led them through the airport to get it.

"I still don't understand why we have to go to some stupid town in Washington instead of going to Disneyland." Mia scowled at Jordan as she seated herself in a booster seat in the mid-sized sedan he'd rented.

"We'll go to Disney next week, okay sweetie?" Jordan glanced at her in the rearview mirror. She'd been griping since last night when they'd told her about the change in vacation plans and he was already tired of the complaints. But he had broken a promise to her, albeit only for a slight shift in timing. He was willing to make allowances for her behavior – at least until his patience ran out, which at this rate would be fairly soon.

"My friend Maura told me that Candle Beach is really awesome." Carrie twisted around in her seat to talk to Mia. "There's a cool park and shops. The next town over has a movie theater and bowling alley, and, of course, there's the beach. I don't think you're going to be bored."

Jordan shot Carrie a grateful smile. "Aunt Carrie's right. You'll love it."

"I doubt it." Mia folded her arms and stared out the window, a scowl marring her face.

He sighed. Yep, his patience was rapidly coming to an end. He flipped on the radio and asked Carrie, "Do you want to choose a station?"

"Sure." She fiddled with the radio but didn't seem satisfied with the choices. "Better yet, I'll link up my phone to it."

He groaned. That meant two hours of listening to her favorite band, the Barenaked Ladies. Still though, he was grateful she'd decided to come with them. He looked back at Mia. Her gaze was locked on something far out the window and she'd put her over-the-ear headphones on, which from experience he knew would block out all sound.

"Do you think this is going to work?" he asked Carrie. "Do you think she'll take me back?"

She shrugged. "I mean, I can't say for sure, but if she's the woman you think she is, she'll listen to reason."

"I hope so." He tightened his grip on the steering wheel. If she didn't, he'd just derailed his relationship with his daughter for nothing. They drove for a while, listening to a constant soundtrack of Barenaked Ladies as the scenery whizzed by. Carrie's eyes were glued to the window. "Have you ever been up to Washington before?"

"Nope." She turned to him for a moment. "We took some family road trips when I was a kid, but it was usually to national parks like Yosemite or the Grand Canyon. We never made it up north to Seattle."

"You'll love it. Candle Beach is gorgeous – both the town and the beach itself. There's something about it that's almost spiritual, like you can stand on the beach and just let the sound and scent of the ocean wash over you and clean your soul." He gave her a wry grin. "Okay, I'm starting to sound like a self-help infomercial."

"Yeah, just a little bit." She laughed. "But I know what you mean. I love being out in nature. And Maura is excited to show me around town. I'll have plenty to do when you and Mia are hanging out with Amelia."

Amelia. He had to force himself to focus on the road as a vision of her popped into his head: her lovely soft brown hair and piercing blue eyes, her sense of humor and contagious laugh that always warmed his heart... A longing came over him and he wished he could make the next hour go by faster.

Soon, however, they were passing Haven Shores. His palms grew sweaty and he lessened his foot's pressure on the gas pedal. What if she didn't want him in her life?

"I think the speed limit is fifty here." Carrie glanced at the mirror on the passenger side. "There's a line of cars behind us."

He reluctantly sped up until they were close to town. "I'll drop you off at Maura's house first. Amelia and I went there for dinner, and I think I remember where it is." That would give him at least thirty minutes for his nerves to settle before he saw Amelia.

Carrie peered at him. "Are you okay? I've never seen you so nervous."

"I'm fine." He breathed deeply, letting the familiar salt air calm him.

They pulled up to the curb outside of Maura's house and Carrie got out, opening the rear passenger door. "I'll take Mia with me so you can have some time alone with Amelia."

Maura waved at them through the window and then came running out to the curb, her dog, Barker, following close at her heels. She gave Carrie a big hug. "I'm so happy you were able to come up with Jordan." She looked at Mia, who was still in the car. "And this must be Mia."

Mia didn't react.

Carrie removed Mia's headphones to address her. "This is my friend Maura. We're going to hang out with her for a little while because your dad has something to take care of."

Mia looked up. "Hi."

"Hi, Mia, nice to meet you." Maura stepped back to allow Mia room to exit the car. Barker bumbled around them, barking excitedly.

Jordan grabbed Carrie's bag from the trunk and rolled it up to the front door. The others followed, with Carrie holding Mia's booster seat.

"I'll be back in a couple hours to take you all to dinner." Jordan gave Mia a hug before she could resist.

"Take all the time you need," Maura said. "We'll have a great time here until you come back." She winked at Mia. "Maybe even get an ice cream cone in town if that's okay with your dad."

Jordan grinned. "An ice cream cone is fine, but don't load her up with too much sugar. I've got something special planned for dinner."

Mia perked up. "What is it, Daddy?"

"It's a surprise," he said.

Mia pouted at him, then walked in front of Carrie to enter Maura's house.

Jordan watched her go. Was she going to be this recalcitrant for the whole trip? He really wanted his daughter to like Amelia, but he was starting to doubt that everything would go according to script.

"She'll be fine." Carrie patted him on the arm. "Now go get your girl."

"Thanks, Carrie."

Jordan stopped at the local market to pick up a bouquet

of red roses, then drove to the Candle Beach Hotel. The entire time, he was running his lines and visualizing how things would go with Amelia, as though he were blocking out a movie – one of the most important films of his entire life. When he was outside of the hotel, he called Aidan, who'd promised to act as a lookout.

"I'm here," Jordan said. "Is Amelia alone?"

"There's a guest in there, but I don't think they'll be long." Aidan paused. "Okay, the coast is clear."

Jordan opened the door to the lobby and walked in. Amelia was sitting behind the front desk, chewing on a stick of red licorice, completely engrossed in something on the computer.

Jordan cleared his throat and she looked up. As soon as she saw him, her face lit up and she jumped out of the chair, dropping the candy on the desk.

"You came back!" She ran toward him, throwing herself at him.

This wasn't how he'd seen things going, but he wasn't complaining. He enveloped her in his arms, then firmly kissed her on the lips. She tasted of red licorice and he felt like he'd come home.

After a few moments, she stepped back. "I didn't know you were coming back to town. Are you staying here? Your name isn't on the guest register."

He laughed. "I am staying here. I used one of the fake names I often use to keep a low profile. Did you see a Bob Brown on the register?"

She grinned. "I did, but I had no idea it was you."

"You don't seem mad at me." He peered at her, holding his breath for her response.

She shook her head. "No. I'm so sorry I didn't call you back. I called you a few days ago and some woman answered – I immediately thought the worst, but I shouldn't have."

"I know. It was my sister-in-law you spoke with."

"I figured it was something like that. I didn't even think about it being Carrie, although I should have. I was so spooked by the long-distance thing that I jumped to the conclusion that it was one of those women the media is always linking you to."

"I told you those stories are blown out of proportion." He brushed a lock of hair out of her face.

"I know." Her eyes met his. "Can you forgive me?"

"Oh, I suppose so." He kissed her again. A flash went off. How had they found him already? He threw himself in front of her to shield her from the paparazzi.

"What are you doing?" she whispered.

"Trying to keep you out of the spotlight," he answered.

She pointed behind him. "Look."

He turned to see who'd been taking pictures of them. Aidan.

Aidan shrugged innocently. "I promised Maura I'd get pictures of the happy couple."

He sighed. "I thought you were paparazzi."

"Sorry." Aidan's eyes sparkled. "Amelia, I'll send Tania in to take over the rest of your shift."

"I thought you said she had the rest of the evening off."

He laughed. "I may have lied a little. I had to make sure you were here when Jordan arrived." He exited into the hallway to the Great Room.

When they were alone, Amelia looked up at Jordan. "Did you come up here by yourself?"

"Nope. Carrie and Mia came up too. Carrie is staying with Maura for the week, but I wanted you to meet her and Mia. They're a big part of my life." He reached for her hands and held them tightly, never wanting to let her go again.

"I know. I'm excited to meet them." She looked directly at him and he felt that almost electric connection pass through them. "Does Mia know about me?"

He sighed and looked down. "Not yet. I figured I'd tell her right before dinner. I have to warn you, she's not too thrilled about being up here. We were supposed to go to Disneyland, and I put it off until next week. I had to see you."

"Ouch. I can see why she'd be upset." She frowned. "She'll probably think I'm the reason why you didn't go this week."

"She'll get over it," he said firmly. "She's only eight, but I swear, she's well on her way to being an angsty teenager. I'll have a talk with her and make her understand that none of this was your doing." He squeezed her hands.

"Okay."

A young woman came in, grinning at them, as though she were in on the whole thing. "I'm here to take over for you at the desk."

Amelia smiled at her. "Thanks, Tania."

"No problem. I'm happy to help." Tania moved past them to take her position behind the front desk.

Amelia and Jordan walked outside together, holding hands.

"Now what?" Amelia asked.

"Now I go back to Maura's house and get everyone, and we come back to have a picnic on the beach together. It'll be fun." He tried to convince himself that his daughter was going to cheerfully go along with the plan, but doubts lingered in his mind.

"I'll head back to my cottage and freshen up for dinner then. Maybe put on something a little more appropriate for dinner on the beach than this." She eyed her black linen pants and button-down silk blouse.

He twirled her around to face him. "I'll see you in about an hour, down on the beach in our spot."

"Our spot," she said, her face glowing. "I like the sound of that."

He left her in front of her cottage, then returned to his rental car, whistling the whole way. Things had gone a little off-script, but he wouldn't have changed a thing.

16

"There's sand on my hotdog," Mia said. "Why'd we have to eat on the beach?"

"Because it's hard to roast hotdogs in a restaurant." Jordan's voice was steady, but Amelia wondered how long he could hold on. Mia had been complaining steadily since Jordan had brought her down to the beach.

Aidan raised an eyebrow and his lips quivered as though he was trying hard not to laugh. Maura nudged him and shook her head almost imperceptibly before handing him a bun for the hot dog he'd just pulled off a charred stick.

Carrie sighed and said to Amelia, "I hear you're an interior designer. That must be fascinating. There are a bunch of houses in our area that I'd love to see the insides of."

"I love being an interior designer," Amelia said. "I get to turn a client's dream rooms into reality." She laughed. "Plus, it *is* fun to see the interior of some of the houses I work with. You wouldn't believe what some of these people have in their homes. One client even had a small creek running through the middle of their house!"

"Wow," Maura said. "That would be amazing."

"A creek? Seriously? I don't believe you." Mia's eyes were heavy on Amelia's face. "Are you making that up?"

"No. There really was a creek in the house. A full-sized tree next to it too." Amelia popped a potato chip into her mouth, savoring the salty treat, the still-warm air, and the joy of being around friends and family.

"Amelia decorated the whole hotel," Aidan said.

"Then I'm sure I won't like it." Mia eyed Amelia defiantly.

Amelia recoiled. Things were not going as well as she'd hoped for with Jordan's daughter. She hadn't expected for Mia to accept her with open arms, but she also hadn't expected such animosity. Why did Mia dislike her so much?

"Mia. That's enough," Jordan said.

Mia glared at him and stalked off toward the water's edge.

He came up behind Amelia and wrapped his arms around her, kissing her cheek. "Sorry she's acting like this," he whispered.

She stiffened at his touch, her gaze darting in Mia's direction. The little girl's attention was on the ocean waves, so she allowed herself to relax into Jordan's arms.

"It's okay. This wasn't what she was expecting." Although she'd wanted to meet Mia, she wished that Jordan had prepared his daughter earlier to meet her. It must have come as a shock to find out that her dad was dating someone and that their dream family vacation had been ripped away for her to come and meet the new woman in his life.

"Still. She shouldn't be behaving like this. I'll have a talk with her." Jordan turned toward his daughter.

"No, you stay here with Amelia." Carrie sighed. "I'll go talk to her." She jogged off in Mia's direction. She stopped beside Mia and put her hand on the little girl's arm. Mia turned to her and they bent their heads down, talking.

What was Carrie saying to her niece? Carrie and Amelia had seemingly gotten along from the start, and she hoped that she hadn't been misreading that situation. If both Carrie and Mia didn't like her, she wasn't sure a relationship with Jordan would work.

"Maybe I should have gone." Jordan moved away from Amelia, gazing at his daughter with a miserable expression on his face. "I never seem to know what to say to her though."

Amelia stood behind him, feeling just as helpless as him.

Carrie came back a few minutes later. "Mia is going to have some alone time until she can figure out how to behave around the rest of us." She turned to Amelia and addressed her directly. "I'm sorry she's been behaving so badly. She's not usually like this."

"It's okay." Amelia's words felt lame, but she didn't know what else to say. Her new boyfriend's child didn't like her and there wasn't much she could do about it.

Maura put the hotdogs back in the cooler. "Anyone want s'mores before all the coals burn out?" She held up a package of marshmallows.

Jordan grinned. "I know I do." He looked down the beach at Mia. "I really wanted Mia to have some. I don't think she's ever had s'mores before."

"I'll go ask her if she wants one." As soon as the words were out of her mouth, Amelia regretted them. Why was she running directly into the lion's den?

He peered at her. "Are you sure?"

She mustered up her best reassuring smile. "Yep. I'll go talk to her." She started down the beach to Mia, her heart beating double-time as she approached the little girl. "Um, your dad wanted to know if you'd like to roast a marshmallow. We're going to have s'mores."

Mia eyed her with more contempt than she'd expect from an eight-year-old. "You're not my mother."

Amelia stepped back and took a deep breath. "I know I'm not your mother. I wasn't trying to be your mother."

"Good." Mia glared at her. "And he's my daddy. He was supposed to take me to Disneyland and now I'm stuck in this stupid town, all because of you."

The venom in her words wounded Amelia, but she tried to conceal how much it hurt. "I'm sorry you feel that way. I didn't ask your dad to come up here."

"Yeah, but he wouldn't have dragged us up here if it weren't for you." Mia took off running back to the campfire.

Amelia followed behind her, allowing the loose sand to slow her steps. Mia joined Carrie and Jordan at the fire, reaching for a marshmallow stick. Jordan held up a hand to shade his eyes and looked in Amelia's direction, but didn't say anything before he helped Mia thread a marshmallow onto the wooden stick.

"Everything okay?" Aidan asked in a low voice as Amelia walked past him.

"Uh-huh," she eked out. Everything was most definitely not okay. She wasn't sure if it would ever be again.

He started to say something but seemed to think better of it. "I'm going to see if Maura needs anything."

Amelia sat down on a beach log a safe distance away to watch the production of s'mores.

Jordan finished roasting a marshmallow and sandwiched it alongside a piece of chocolate between two graham crackers. He walked over to where Amelia sat alone, holding out the treat. "Do you want one?"

She shook her head. Being around Mia had made her appetite disappear.

He shrugged and bit into the s'more, causing melted marshmallow to ooze out the sides and onto his chin. Without thinking she reached out to brush it away. He smiled at her and her insides melted along with the marshmallow.

He popped the last bite into his mouth and brushed off his hands. "It looked like the two of you had a good talk down by the water."

She lifted an eyebrow. Had he seen the same conversation she'd taken part in? On the other hand, she didn't want to tell him that Mia hated her and thought she was there to replace her mother.

"We talked a little." She eyed Mia with her peripheral vision. Mia was shooting daggers back at her. Amelia bit her lip and forced herself to ignore her.

"Well, that's a start." He leaned over and kissed her, then checked his watch. "It's getting to be Mia's bedtime. I'd better get her back to the room and ready for bed. She's already feeling a little off-kilter, so I'd like to stick to her normal schedule as much as possible."

Amelia nodded. "I think that's a good idea."

Jordan and Mia said goodnight to everyone, then left for the hotel. After they'd separated the coals to prevent any unintended fires, Amelia helped Carrie, Maura, and Aidan carry the cooler and bags of food back to the hotel as well.

When the sun had faded beyond the horizon and Carrie and Maura had gone back to Maura's house, Aidan and Amelia sat together on the deserted front porch, chatting quietly.

"I think Mia hates me," Amelia admitted.

Aidan became fascinated with a small pile of sand on one of the deck boards.

"Aidan!"

He looked up. "I'm sure she doesn't hate you."

"It certainly seemed like it." Her stomach churned, remembering Mia accusing her of trying to replace her mother.

He turned in his chair to face her. "Look, Jordan has baggage. He's got a little girl who's desperately missing her mother. It's going to take time."

"I know," she whispered. "I just wish she'd give me a chance."

"Give it time." He stood and patted her on the shoulder. "She's hurting and thinks you're trying to take her father away from her. Help her realize that you're not going to do that."

"How?"

He laughed lightly. "Heck if I know. I don't have a lot of experience with little kids either. I'm sure you'll figure it out though." He slipped back into the hotel, leaving Amelia alone on the deck.

She pulled her knees up to her chest, hugging them tightly. She had to figure out a way to get through to Mia. If she couldn't forge a friendship with her, she wouldn't be able to keep Jordan, and that wasn't an option.

Amelia sat on the sofa in her cottage the afternoon after the beach cookout, working out her finances so she'd be prepared when she and Charlotte toured the retail space the next day. She'd met Jordan and Mia for a late breakfast at the Bluebonnet Cafe, but the little girl hadn't magically warmed to her overnight and things had been awkward. Father and daughter had headed out for a beach walk soon after, leaving her time to get some work done. Charlotte had sent her what she knew about the terms of the lease, and while finances would be tight until her interior design business was up and running, it was doable.

A knock sounded on the door and Amelia looked up. "Who is it?"

"It's me, Tania. It's kind of an emergency."

Amelia jumped up from the couch and flung the door open. "What's wrong? Is someone hurt?" Had something happened to Jordan or Aidan?

Tania's face was red. "No, no. Everyone is fine. There's a plumbing emergency."

Amelia allowed herself to breathe again. "Okay. Did you call the handyman?"

The new employee nodded. "I called Elvis and Aidan. No one is answering. I'm sorry for bothering you, but I didn't know who else to call."

"Don't worry about it. I don't mind. What seems to be the problem?" Amelia grabbed her keys and locked the cottage as she followed Tania back to the hotel.

"There's water leaking through the ceiling into room 126. A lot of water. The housekeeper found it like that when she went in there to clean. I ran upstairs to see where it was coming from, and found the toilet overflowing in room 226. I turned off the water to the toilet, but it's a horrible mess and I wasn't sure what to do."

Amelia stared at her. Jordan and Mia were staying in room 226. "Can you show me, please?"

Tania nodded sharply and held up a plastic key card. "I've got a key with me."

When they were standing in front of Jordan's room, Amelia rapped on the door. No one answered, so they let themselves in. Sure enough, the entire floor of the bathroom was soaked, as was the carpet nearby. Amelia crossed the wet floor to examine the toilet. A hand towel had been stuffed into the bowl to plug it.

"Someone did this on purpose," she said. And she had a feeling she knew who'd done it.

"Yeah. That's what I figured." Tania shifted between her feet. "I should probably get back to the front desk now. Are you okay with all of this?"

Amelia sighed. "Yeah. I'll take care of it. You can go back to the desk."

Tania left her alone with the clogged toilet and water-logged floor. Amelia pulled out her phone and speed-dialed the handyman.

He answered almost as soon as the call connected. "Hey, I saw I'd missed a call from the hotel, and I was just about to give you a ring. I was knee-deep in sewer water when you called."

Amelia grimaced. That was an image she didn't need in her brain. "We've got a bit of a problem here at the hotel. One of the toilets overflowed and everything in that room and the one below it is soaked."

"I'll be right there." He hung up the phone.

"Why are you in my room?" Jordan's voice rang out. "And why's it so wet in here?"

She whirled around to face him. "Someone stuffed a hand towel into the toilet and it overflowed. It was probably running for a while."

Concern flickered in his eyes as he made his way into the bathroom to investigate. "Maybe it just fell in there."

"That didn't just fall in there. It's wedged tightly in the toilet's drain." She leaned against the sink. "Someone did it on purpose."

"You think Mia did it?" He ran his fingers through his hair.

"Unless you did?" She tried hard to keep the frustration out of her voice, but a little seeped through.

"She was in the bathroom right before we left. Said

something about wanting to pull her hair back so it wouldn't get tangled in the wind." He looked at Amelia. "I can't believe she'd do something like this though."

"I can," Amelia said. "She was pretty upset with me yesterday. She probably figured this was a good way of getting back at me."

He closed his eyes for a moment and leaned against the door, folding his arms across his chest. "I'm so sorry about this. I'll cover the cost of any damages, of course."

"Our insurance should cover most of it, but I'm hoping that the handyman will be able to get things dried out by evening, or you won't have a room to stay in." She looked past him. "Where is Mia anyway?"

"I dropped her off with Carrie before we came back. They're going to see a movie with Maura in Haven Shores."

Elvis came into the room, making noises under his breath as he surveyed the damage. "I'll get the fans in here, and these thin carpets should dry quickly, but I checked out the room below this one already and repairing the ceiling and walls in there is going to take a few days at minimum."

Amelia groaned. "I'll try to get ahold of Aidan to figure out if we can shift some guests around. Thanks for coming so quickly."

"No problem. I'm going to go get started on the room downstairs." He walked out of the room, letting the door shut behind him.

"I don't even know what to say," Jordan said. "I can't believe Mia would do something like this." Bewilderment flickered in his eyes. "What happened to my sweet little girl?"

"I think this has all been a little much for her." Amelia stared at the mess, then sent Aidan a quick text to let him know about the incident and that she had things handled for the meantime.

"I don't care if she's upset; this is not okay." Jordan gritted his teeth and pulled out his phone, jabbing at the screen with his index finger, then held it to his ear. "Hi, Carrie. It's me. I need you to bring Mia back here." He stopped to listen to whatever she was saying.

"I know. I'll explain it to you later, but I need to talk to her right now about something she did." He hung up the phone and turned to Amelia. "I'm so sorry about this. Is there anything I can do to help while I'm waiting for Mia? They left for Haven Shores about ten minutes ago, but Carrie's going to turn around and bring Mia back here."

She looked around. "Grab a towel, I guess. I'll get the mop out of the cleaning cart." They mopped up the mess until someone knocked on the hotel room door.

Jordan flung it open. Carrie stood in the doorway with her hands on the shoulders of a very sullen-looking Mia. Maura hovered just behind them.

"What did she do?" Carrie asked. "She admitted to doing something wrong, but she won't tell me what."

Jordan pointed at the bathroom and Mia squirmed. "Somebody decided it was a good idea to stuff a towel into the toilet and flush it. The whole room below us is flooded."

Carrie's face turned ashen as she turned to face her niece. "Mia!"

Amelia hung back, not sure if she should say anything.

Jordan looked down at his daughter. "Why did you do this? This is going to cost a fortune to repair."

She eyed him defiantly. "It's Amelia's hotel, right?" She glanced over at Amelia and sneered at her. "Now we can't stay here."

Jordan sighed. "I don't understand why you'd want to cause damage to the hotel."

Mia shrugged. "I just did. I don't want to stay in her hotel."

"This is unacceptable," Jordan said. "Amelia hasn't done anything to you. If you had a problem, you should have come to me."

"If it wasn't for her, we'd be at Disneyland right now." Tears glistened in her eyes.

"Well, this little antic of yours has lost you any chance of going to Disneyland this summer," he said quietly.

Mia glared at her father. "I hate her. And I hate you! I never want to see you again." She ran out of the room. Carrie and Maura rushed after her.

Jordan's back heaved as he watched his little girl run away. Amelia bit her lip and tried to make herself one with the wall. It was worse than she'd thought. Now not only did Mia hate her, but she was angry at her father as well.

It was all Amelia's fault. If she'd never come into Jordan's life, Mia's life wouldn't have been disrupted. Mia needed the stability of having her father home with her and knowing that she came first in his life. With Amelia in the picture, Mia would need to share him. Amelia's own parents had been a huge influence on her, and she didn't know what she'd do without them. Mia was already down one parent and couldn't afford to lose another.

"Jordan – are you okay?" Amelia asked.

He turned around, as if just remembering she was still there. "Yeah. I'm fine." He looked as though he'd aged ten years in the last ten minutes. Amelia crossed the soggy carpet and gave him a hug, then stepped back. His face was etched with pain and indecision.

"Should I go after her?" he asked, looking toward the hallway.

"I don't know." Amelia followed his gaze, but Mia was long gone. She didn't know much about children, but she could imagine how Mia must be feeling at the moment and she knew what she needed to do. "Jordan. We need to talk."

His head snapped around to see her. "What is it?"

She fought to hold back the tidal wave of emotions that was crashing over her. "I don't think this is going to work out between the two of us."

"What do you mean?" He motioned to the bathroom. "Because of what Mia did? I can pay for the damages, and she'll be punished." He shook his head. "I still can't believe she'd play a trick like this."

Amelia put a hand on his arm. "She's hurting."

"Her mom's been gone for two years." He sighed. "I thought she was doing better."

"No. She's afraid of losing you too. Why else would she be doing this?" Amelia picked up the sodden towels and piled them in the bathtub. From the room below them came the sounds of an industrial-strength fan revving up.

"So she's upset. I'll make it right with her." His eyes locked with hers. "I can't afford to lose you."

"And I can't come between you and your daughter," she said. "This just isn't going to work between us."

"Don't I get a say in this?" he asked, his voice full of desperation.

"No. I can't be the one that ruins your relationship with your daughter. She needs you." Before she lost her nerve, she stood on her tiptoes and kissed his cheek, whispering into his ear, "I love you." She ran out of the room and made it all the way to her cottage before the tears broke loose, washing over her cheeks and down her neck as she slumped into the couch cushions.

17

Jordan woke up the next morning on the couch in the owner's suite. Aidan had graciously put him and Mia up in his private suite for the night while their room was drying out. Jordan slid his feet onto the ground and stood, stretching his arms out high above him. Sleeping on the couch had been like sleeping on a cement slab, and he felt as though he'd been hit by a Mack truck.

How had things with Amelia deteriorated so quickly? One minute they'd been blissfully happy, and the next, she was breaking up with him. He eyed the closed bedroom door where Mia was sleeping in Amelia's old room. He'd never expected his daughter would react the way she did or do what she did. She'd cried herself to sleep last night, whether because he'd taken away the Disney trip or because he was angry with her, he didn't know.

Jordan opened the door and walked over to the bed. Mia lay there, her hair strewn about the pillow and her stuffed elephant hugged tightly to her chest. She looked like an angel. All of his anger dissolved.

Had Amelia been right to break up with him? He knew he needed to spend more time with Mia, but he could accomplish that as well as have Amelia in his life if he chose not to take on the movie role he'd auditioned for. They were both so important to him.

He sat in a chair nearby and waited for fifteen minutes until Mia woke up.

She opened her eyes. "Daddy?"

He nodded and scooted the chair closer to her. "Did you want to get up and have some breakfast with me? They have really good apple fritters here. I know how much you love them."

She eyed him warily and said in a little voice, "Aren't you still mad at me?"

He sighed. "I'm still mad about the choice you made to damage the hotel. But no matter what you do, I'll always love you."

"So, we can go to Disneyland now?" she asked, sitting up in bed.

"Nope. That's still off the table. There have to be some consequences for your actions."

"Oh." She hugged her stuffed animal. "Okay." She looked up at him. "I didn't know the water would go all the way to the room downstairs from us." She pressed her lips together. "I just thought it would get on our floor and we'd have to leave. When the toilet at home got plugged, it only overflowed a little bit before Aunt Carrie fixed it."

He ran a hand through his hair. "Sometimes things don't turn out exactly how we intended."

"Yeah." She rubbed her hand across the elephant's back, ruffling its gray plush fur. "Are Amelia and her brother mad at me?"

"I don't know," he said truthfully. "I haven't talked to either of them today." He leaned forward in his chair. "And I don't think we'll be seeing much of them in the future." Pain shot through him at the thought of never seeing Amelia again.

Mia looked up at him sharply. "What do you mean? Is Amelia mad at you?"

"No, sweetie." He stood and paced the floor in front of her bed. "Amelia decided that this wasn't a good time for us to be dating because it upset you so much." His stomach twisted, and he turned to the wall to rest his head against it, hoping to stabilize his thoughts.

"Oh." Mia was quiet. "Daddy? Did you love her?"

He looked at her sadly. "Yeah. I think I did." He took a deep breath and went over to his daughter, kissing her on the forehead. "But that's in the past now. I'm going to go take a shower and then we'll head out to breakfast, okay?"

She nodded. "Okay, Daddy."

He left the room and gathered up everything he'd need for the shower. Although he felt horrible, he wasn't mad at Mia. She'd acted out because she was too young to fully express her feelings about her dad dating someone other than her mom. Not that his relationship with Amelia was an issue anymore. She'd made it clear that she couldn't be with him because she didn't want to come between him and Mia.

He'd do anything to change her mind, but although he hadn't known Amelia long, he knew her well enough to know how stubborn she was and unlikely to change her mind about him. He'd brought Mia here to meet Amelia, hoping his daughter would fall in love with her, just like he had. Could he have done something differently that would have changed the outcome?

~

Jordan leaned back on the park bench, watching his daughter pump her legs to swing higher and higher. The air was thick with the scent of recent rain and a slight breeze rustled the leaves in the tree branches overhead.

"What are you going to do about Amelia?" Carrie asked.

He pulled his attention away from Mia. "I don't know if there's anything I can do." He shrugged. "She made her decision and she's not one to change her mind."

"And you're just going to let her do that?" Carrie shook her head. "I thought *you* were more stubborn than that. The Jordan Rivers I know would never let someone he loved slip away without a fight, and he certainly wouldn't choose to check out early to avoid any chance of getting her back."

He stared in the direction of the ocean, something he'd forevermore associate with Amelia and the long walks they'd taken together on the beach. "Mia doesn't like her and there's not much I can do about that."

"She's eight. She changes her mind about twenty times a day." She wiped at some water on the bench with the towel they'd brought to dry off the swings from that morning's rainstorm. "Look, I know I've been after you to spend more time with Mia, but this doesn't feel right. I'd give anything to bring Annie back, but that's not happening. She'll always have a special place in your hearts, but for both your and Mia's sakes, you need to move forward with your lives."

"You think I should try to talk Amelia into giving me another chance?" His hopes lifted, then sank as fast as his daughter on a downward swing. "She'll never do it."

"Why?"

"Amelia and Aidan's parents died a few years ago. Both of them were close to their parents and took their deaths really hard. I think Amelia feels like she understands Mia and she doesn't want Mia to have to compete with her for my attention."

"Oh." Carrie glanced at Mia and then turned her attention back to Jordan. "I didn't know about her parents."

"Yeah." Jordan ran his fingers over the side of the rough wooden bench. "The recent loss of a loved one was one of the things we bonded over." He laughed nervously. "Weird, I know."

"No, it makes sense." Carrie looked at him. "After Annie died, I attended some group grief-counseling sessions. A few of the women I met there are good friends of mine now." She sighed. "I can tell how much you like her. We don't leave until tomorrow. I think you should try to talk to Mia about Amelia before we go. Or I can talk to her about it if you'd like."

He stared at his daughter. "No, I'd better be the one to do it. But thank you."

She nodded. "Let me know if there's anything I can do to help." She stood from the bench. "I have plans to meet Maura for lunch since it's our last day here. I'll see you for dinner, okay?"

"Have fun." He watched Carrie as she walked off down the street in the direction of Maura's house. He loved how everything was so close together in Candle Beach. On most days here, you wouldn't even need a car. He spent so much time in gridlocked traffic that the idea of being within walking distance to home, his daughter's school, and everything else sounded wonderful. But his career wasn't here. He still needed to make some decisions about that.

"Daddy?" Mia said.

He turned to find her standing only a foot away.

"Can we go to the beach? I didn't get a chance to build a sandcastle yet."

"Sure, sweetie. Let's stop at the hotel first and get a bucket and shovel. Aidan said they have them for guests to use."

"Do we have to go back to the hotel?" she asked.

"Yeah, why?"

"Amelia might be there." She looked at the ground.

"She might." He peered at her face. "Is that a problem?"

"She must be mad at me." Mia chewed on her bottom lip.

"I don't think she's mad at you." He sighed. "Mia, we need to talk about Amelia." He guided her over to the bench to sit next to him.

"Okay," she said quietly.

"I really care about Amelia, but no matter how I feel about her, I'll always love you. You know that, right?"

"I know, Daddy." She didn't make eye contact with him. "But she's not my mommy." Her eyes filled with tears and he wrapped her in his arms.

"No, she's not your mom. But I do think your mom would have liked her." He pulled away and looked at her, mopping her face with the bottom of his shirt. "Do you think you can make an effort to be nice to her?"

Mia stiffened. "I thought you weren't dating her anymore."

He took a steeling breath. "I'm not. But I'd like for her to be a part of both of our lives."

"No." She jumped off the bench and ran over to the base of a tree. "I don't want her in our lives."

He counted to three, then followed her. He didn't want to pressure Mia, but he wanted her to give Amelia a fair shot, and they were running out of time.

"Okay. But this isn't the last time we're going to talk about this." He reached for her little hand and wrapped it in his. "Now, let's go to the beach and build the biggest sand-castle you've ever seen."

She looked up at him and smiled, melting his heart. He gripped her hand even tighter. He had to figure out a way to have both Mia and Amelia in his life.

18

Amelia sat on the sofa in her cottage, curled up with a warm fleece blanket and a cup of hot tea, watching an old movie on the TV. Usually after a breakup, she'd indulge in a pint of ice cream, but she hadn't wanted to leave her cottage and risk accidentally seeing Jordan. The weather outside perfectly matched her mood – gray and rainy. She sipped her tea, trying to break herself out of the funk she'd been in since she'd spoken with Jordan the night before.

Someone rapped on the window next to the door and Aidan's face appeared.

She unwrapped the blanket from around her legs, stood, and walked over to the door to open it. "Hi."

"Hey. How are you doing?" Aidan's words were soft, but his eyes were heavy on her face. He held a gallon of Rocky Road ice cream in his hands.

She looked pointedly at the ice cream. "Is that for me?"

He stretched his arms out long to offer it to her, probably afraid she'd bite him if he said no. "Maura brought it over for you."

She got a spoon out of a kitchen drawer and dug into the frozen treat. "Please thank her for me." She trudged back to the couch and recovered herself with the blanket's comforting weight.

He nodded. "Is there anything I can do?"

"Nope. And don't worry, I won't be like this all day. Charlotte and I are meeting with the owner of the building across the street from her shop this evening. If he likes us and we like the space, we're hoping to sign the papers today." She shoveled a huge spoonful of Rocky Road into her mouth, savoring the creamy sweetness.

"That's great." He hugged her. "Seriously. I'm so happy you've decided to go through with the art gallery and interior design business."

"I still feel a little bad about leaving you in the lurch." She leaned back on the couch and scooped out more ice cream.

"You're not. Tania is working out great," he said firmly. "I'm technically supposed to be at the front desk right now, so I'd better get back, but I wanted to see how you were doing."

"I've been better." She stared into the Rocky Road carton. The mini marshmallows reminded her of Jordan eating a s'more and she put the spoon down. She looked up at Aidan. "Have you talked to Jordan at all?"

Something crossed his face, but she wasn't sure what it was. "I have. He's planning on checking out tomorrow."

She nodded sharply. "Good. You may not see much of me until then because I'm trying to avoid him."

"Oh, Amelia." He sighed. "I wish things had turned out better for the two of you. Are you sure there isn't a chance to work things out?"

She looked out the window. "I can't get between him and his daughter. If she won't accept me, I'm not going to press the issue. She needs Jordan more than I do." Emotion squeezed her heart and she struggled to breathe for a moment.

"I think I understand where you're coming from," Aidan said. "But that doesn't mean I agree with it. Relationships are hard."

"I know. And that's why I can't get in the way of his relationship with Mia." She set the ice cream carton down on the coffee table in front of her. "I've made my decision."

"Then I won't try to dissuade you." He started for the door, pausing in the doorframe. "Let me know if there's anything Maura and I can do for you."

"I will."

He closed the door behind him, and she got up to lock the door. Melted ice cream was beginning to pool in the carton, so she put the lid back on and stuck it in the freezer and the spoon in the sink. Every bone in her body wanted to collapse on the sofa, but she made herself go into the bathroom and take a shower.

The shower helped a little, and by the time she was due to meet Charlotte, she was ready to face the outside world, although it still felt as though a piece of her had been shattered. At least the rain had finally stopped. She drove to Whimsical Delights, Charlotte's knickknack shop located in an old Airstream trailer, and parked just down the road from it.

Charlotte was busy rearranging a family of brightly hued flamingo lawn statues when she arrived. Amelia's feet crunched on the oyster-shell path, causing Charlotte to look up.

"Hey, there you are. I wasn't sure you'd make it today."

She'd just broken up with Jordan the night before. News got around this town fast. "Of course I'd be here." She smiled at Charlotte. "This is going to be an amazing opportunity for both of us."

"That's the spirit." Charlotte placed two larger flamingos next to a set of two smaller birds gathered around a wooden flower. "Actually, the property owner called me this morning to change our appointment time. He's running a little late today. I convinced him to send me the official lease documents though, if you'd like to go over them beforehand."

"Sure." Amelia looked around. Charlotte didn't exactly have an office. "Do you want to do it here?"

"I was thinking about going to Donut Daze for a pre-dinner snack. It's right down the street. Let me tell my assistant I'm leaving." She opened the trailer door and said something to an unseen person, then returned with a file folder in her hand. "Okay. Let's go."

They walked over to the donut shop and sat down together with a donut and cup of coffee each.

Charlotte spread the lease papers over the unused portion of tabletop, pointing at a line near the top of one. "The terms look good to me. What do you think?"

Amelia picked up the piece of paper and scanned the contents for a few minutes. "I think it looks good for the most part. I want to see the inside of the space before I commit to anything though."

"Of course." Charlotte checked her watch. "We've got about ten minutes before we're supposed to be there."

Amelia stood. "I'm ready."

Charlotte looked at her in surprise. "Don't you want to finish your donut?"

Amelia picked up the half-eaten donut and almost-full coffee cup. She'd already consumed way too much sugar for the day and was starting to feel ill. "I don't really feel like it."

Charlotte frowned. "I'm sorry. I wish we could do this on a different day, but this is our last chance. He already has at least two other people seriously looking at the space. If it wasn't for him being a friend of Parker's, he probably wouldn't have bothered with us."

"I didn't exactly see this coming either." Amelia's lips quivered and tears slipped from her eyes. "After Jordan left Candle Beach, I realized I'd fallen in love with him. I never thought things would go bad between us so quickly."

Charlotte hugged her. "I've been there before. Let's go to our meeting. I bet seeing the space will cheer you up."

"I hope so."

They walked down the street to a group of retail spaces across from Charlotte's shop, stopping in front of the one on the end with a "For Lease" sign in the window. A few minutes later, a portly gentleman stepped out of a car and met them at the door with a key in hand.

"Good evening, Charlotte," he said. "I apologize for being so tardy. My afternoon appointments went over their allotted timeslots."

"No problem." She shook his hand. "We're eager to see the space." She turned to Amelia. "This is my business partner, Amelia. Amelia, Mr. Dorton."

"Nice to meet you." Amelia reached out and shook his hand firmly.

He opened the door and ushered them inside. "This is one big room, but we can divide it in two with full-height room dividers. There's also a fairly big office in the back, along with a bathroom and kitchenette."

Both women walked around the room.

"I love the high walls," Charlotte whispered to Amelia.

"I know. And the lighting in here is fantastic." Amelia could already see exactly where she'd put all of the lamps and other items she planned to sell. "And there's a corner of the office that is perfect for my fabric samples."

Mr. Dorton cleared his throat. "What do you think?"

Charlotte looked at Amelia, who nodded.

"We'll take it," Charlotte said in a professional tone, although Amelia could tell she was squealing with excitement inside.

He nodded. "Excellent. Let me get the paperwork out of my car."

He exited the building and Charlotte let out her pent-up squeal.

Amelia grinned and gave her a big hug. "This is going to be awesome for both of us."

Charlotte beamed. "We'll be the one-stop shop for decor that Gretchen wanted. I hope she's right that there will be a market for it."

"There will be." Amelia's phone buzzed and she withdrew it from her purse. Jordan?

She hesitated for a moment, then tapped the button to take the call.

"Amelia," he said. "Mia's missing."

"What?"

Mr. Dorton came back in and walked over to a countertop nearby, dropping the paperwork on it. Amelia moved to the opposite side of the room to hear Jordan better.

"I can't find Mia. I left her alone in the room while I was taking a quick shower to wash off all the sand and when I came out of the bathroom, she was gone. She left a note that said she was running away."

Her heart almost stopped, but she tried to keep calm. "I'm sure she hasn't gone far."

"I don't know what to do. I've looked all over for her. If I call the police, the press will get ahold of this and then she'll be in the spotlight. I can't let that happen."

She took a deep breath, and Charlotte shot her a confused look. "I'm in town right now, but I can be there in five minutes."

"Okay. I'll wait here in case she comes back."

Amelia hung up, then looked up at Charlotte. "I'm so sorry, but I have to go."

"What's wrong?"

Mr. Dorton sighed loudly. "Ma'am, I really need you to sign the papers now. If I can't get your signatures today, I have another client ready to sign."

Amelia locked eyes with Charlotte. "Jordan's daughter is missing – she ran away, and he can't find her. She's only eight."

"Oh my gosh. He must be so scared." Charlotte looked at Mr. Dorton, then back at Amelia. "Go help him. I'll figure this out."

Amelia nodded sharply. "Thank you." She ran out of the building and jumped in her car, driving as fast as she could back to the hotel.

19

Aidan met her in the parking lot. "We've done a quick search of the building, but there's no sign of Mia. We're going to spread out and look through all of the buildings on the grounds, the beach, and along the road to town." They walked quickly together to the hotel lobby, where Jordan was pacing the floor.

"Maura is checking the outbuildings and Carrie's going to take the path along the road." Jordan swallowed hard. "While Aidan checks the guestrooms, can you please take the beach? I'm going to stay here in case she comes back." His eyes were filled with worry. She wanted to stay and comfort him, but she knew they needed to find Mia before it got dark.

She settled for a quick hug, then returned to her cottage to swap out her high-heeled professional shoes for sneakers and ran down to the beach. The sun hadn't set yet and there was plenty of light. Plenty of light to see that the beach stretched on and on as far as the eye could see. About thirty minutes had passed since Jordan had found Mia missing, meaning she'd most likely been gone longer than that. If she'd headed immediately for the beach, she could be miles away at this point.

Think, Amelia. If she were a little kid, unfamiliar with the area, where would she have gone to sulk? She eyed the shore. The driftwood fort she'd seen on her daily beach walks seemed to beckon to her. That's where she'd go if she was a kid who needed some time alone.

She jogged down the beach, scanning the sand for Mia, all the way from the water to the cliffs. She slowed as she approached the fort. It was one of the largest she'd ever seen, with two wide beach logs as a base, and a roof made out of smaller pieces of driftwood. Somebody had spent a lot of time on it.

She ducked down in the entrance, allowing her eyes to adjust to the sudden darkness created by the roof. The sand had been dug out underneath, forming a pit tall enough for her to stand in.

"Mia?" she called out.

No answer. When she could see better, her heart sank. The room was empty. Mia wasn't there. She sat down on the cool sand to think. Where else would a little kid go?

From behind her, someone started sobbing. Amelia whirled around. Where was that coming from?

"Mia?" She crawled on her hands and knees to the shortest portion of the fort. Here, the room turned and opened up into an alcove that had been dug out to the sitting height of an adult.

And Mia was there – sitting with her back against a log, her arms wrapped around a ragged gray elephant. She looked up when Amelia came near. "Why are you here?" she asked.

Amelia took a seat about a foot away from her. "Because everyone is looking for you. Your dad is terrified."

"I left a note." She eyed Amelia defiantly.

Amelia sighed. "Yeah. But that didn't make anyone less worried. An eight-year-old shouldn't be out alone in a strange place."

"I'm just fine."

"Okay, maybe now you are." She looked around. "But I don't see a flashlight – or food. In a few hours, it's going to get dark down on the beach and you won't be able to see anything. Plus, it's dinner time and you'll be mighty hungry."

Mia squirmed. "How dark?"

"Pitch black," Amelia said. "The first time I met your dad, he was down on the beach at night. He had a flashlight, but he was still a little unsure how to get back to the hotel. I had to help him find his way back." She smiled, thinking about the first evening she'd spent with Jordan.

Mia watched her closely. "You really like my dad, don't you."

"I do." Amelia picked up a handful of sand and let it sift through her fingers. "But I don't want to come between the two of you. I know you have a special relationship."

"My mom died," Mia said.

"I know." Amelia focused on the little girl. "And that's why it's important for you to have a good relationship with your dad. Your dad probably didn't mention it to you, but my parents died a few years ago."

"They did?" Mia's eyes were wide.

Amelia nodded, smiling sadly. "My mom and dad were always there for me and my brother. I have to admit; I've been a little lost without them."

"That's how I feel." Mia drew circles in the sand. "Daddy was always gone, and my mom and I did everything together. I know Aunt Carrie tries, but she's not my mom."

"No one will ever take her place," Amelia said. "But you've got a lot of people in your life who love you, especially your dad and Aunt Carrie. They'd do anything for you."

"I know." Mia started to say something else, then stopped.

Amelia glanced at her watch. She'd left Jordan at the hotel over twenty minutes ago. She needed to let him know Mia was safe.

"Can I let your dad know that you're okay?"

Mia looked at her elephant and then nodded. "You can tell him."

Amelia quickly texted Jordan and let him know she'd bring Mia back to him as soon as possible.

"My daddy loves you," Mia blurted out.

Amelia's eyes widened. "Uh…"

"He's sad now." She rubbed one of the elephant's floppy ears.

Amelia took a deep breath. She wasn't sure how much to say to Mia about why she and Jordan had broken up. "I know. I didn't want things to end with him, but it was for the best." She leaned forward to sit up on her knees. "Are you ready to get back to him? Honestly, I didn't bring a flashlight either and I don't want to get caught out here without one when it gets dark. I'm a little scared of the dark."

Mia nodded and let Amelia lead her out of the fort.

"Is Daddy going to be mad at me?" she asked.

On impulse, Amelia hugged her. "No, honey. I think he's just going to be happy to see you. Everyone will be."

Mia surprised her by wrapping her little arms around Amelia's waist, then reaching up for Amelia's hand. Was she warming to her? Amelia didn't say anything about it but held Mia's hand until they reached the narrow stairs up from the beach.

~

Jordan was waiting at the top of the stairs and swooped in to grab Mia as soon as they were on the hotel grounds. What if something had happened to her? She could have gotten lost, or kidnapped, or anything. He held her tightly against him, until she cried out.

"Daddy, you're squishing me!"

He immediately loosened his grip. "Sorry, sweetie. I was just so worried."

"I'm fine, Daddy." Mia stepped back.

"I know." He hugged her again, this time more gently, then looked up at Amelia. "Thank you, Amelia."

She nodded. "Of course. I'm glad we found her so quickly."

"Me too." He didn't know what he would have done if they hadn't found Mia soon. He'd been starting to get a little crazy at the thought of losing her.

Carrie came over and hugged Mia too, then shook her finger at her. "Don't ever do that to us again." She choked on her words and then kissed Mia's head. "We were so worried."

"Sorry, Aunt Carrie." Mia hung her head, as if finally realizing how stressful her disappearance had been on her family.

Amelia watched for a few minutes, then slipped away, heading back down to the beach. Jordan called out for her, but she didn't hear him with the wind along the cliff.

Carrie tapped him on the shoulder. "Go after her."

He stared at Mia. "But Mia..."

"She'll be fine. Go get Amelia." Carrie gently turned his shoulders toward the beach.

"Daddy!" Mia said.

He pivoted rapidly. She'd just come back. He shouldn't leave his daughter, but he didn't want to lose Amelia either. His head swam with indecision. "What, sweetie?"

"I love you, Daddy." She ran up to him and hugged him. "Amelia isn't so bad. And I think she has a crush on you!"

He kissed the top of her head. "I love you too, sweetie."

"Go get her before it gets dark!" she told him. "She doesn't like the dark either."

He grinned. "I'll keep that in mind." He kissed her again and hurried after Amelia.

He found her sitting on the sand in their spot, her back to the cliff. He watched her for a moment as she gazed out at the ocean, the last remnants of sun reflecting off of her windswept hair. She had her knees to her chest and a pensive look on her face.

"Penny for your thoughts?" he asked.

Her head whipped around. "What are you doing here? How's Mia? She seemed like she was feeling a little better by the time I left."

He sat down next to her on the soft sand. "Mia's fine. She's with Carrie and Maura."

"Shouldn't you be with her?" Amelia peered into his eyes. "I don't want her getting more upset because you're down here with me."

"Actually, she told me to follow you down here."

Amelia's eyes widened. "She did? Why?"

He shrugged. "You must have made quite an impression on her when you found her."

"I talked to her a little about losing my own mom and dad, but I told her I wasn't going to interfere with her relationship with you." She moved back a few inches and turned to face him. "I wanted to make sure she knows that she comes first with you."

"She knows. But I think she also realizes that I need you in my life too."

"Really?" A small smile crossed Amelia's lips. "Do you think she'll accept me?"

"She told me to come find you. I think you're in." He laughed. "Well, if you don't interfere with any future Disney trips. That could be a deal breaker."

She laughed and slugged him lightly on the arm. "I think I can manage that." She sobered. "But what about your career? I'm planning on starting my interior design business up here and sharing a space with Charlotte. I can't just pick up and leave. Although, I guess I never did sign the lease agreement, so we'll probably lose that space." She sighed. "And it was so perfect. But there will be other places to lease."

He stared at her. "What do you mean you didn't sign the lease agreement? Why not?"

"I was just about to sign, and I got the call from you about Mia running away. I left immediately."

"So you may have lost the place because of me?"

She shook her head. "It was my decision. You and Mia are important to me. Like I said, if it was meant to be, we'll get it. If not, there will be other places."

He was filled suddenly with a mix of emotions, mainly love with a streak of guilt running through it. If he'd been the reason for Amelia to lose her dream property, he'd never forgive himself. But she'd given it up to help him find Mia. That said a lot about her and how committed she was to him and his daughter.

He looked up, focusing on the horizon as the sun sank lower in the sky. "I'm not going to take the role."

"What? Why?" she asked. "This was a dream role for you, right?"

"I don't want to lose the time with you and Mia."

"It's what, eight weeks?" She shook her head. "Nope. We'll be here for you when you get back. If after filming is over you still feel the same about quitting acting, fine. But give this role a chance."

"But I won't see you until summer's over then."

"Perfect. I promised Aidan I'd help out a little at the hotel during the tourist season and I need to get my business up and running. After the summer rush at the hotel, I'll come and visit you. Maybe you and Mia can come up here during one of her breaks from school."

"It would make it a lot easier if we just moved up here."

Her eyes were heavy on his face. "Not that I don't want you to move up here, but isn't that kind of sudden? Mia has friends at school, right?"

"She does, but she'll make new friends." He stopped talking, wanting to see how he felt about this sudden decision. He wasn't used to making quick decisions, but this one felt like a slam dunk. He wanted Mia to grow up in a small town like Candle Beach and be away from all the bad influences in the Hollywood scene. But who'd help with her? He couldn't ask Carrie to move away from L.A. She'd already done enough for them.

"How about we table that decision until later in the summer." Amelia snuggled closer to him. "You can find out how Mia and Carrie feel about it."

He reached over and smoothed her hair away from her cheeks, then gently kissed her on the lips. "I think that sounds like a wonderful idea."

CHAPTER 20 AND AUTHOR'S NOTE

Two weeks after Jordan, Mia, and Carrie left to go home to Los Angeles, Amelia was back in the swing of things. With a little cajoling from Charlotte, Mr. Dorton had given them the lease and they'd started preparing the space for their business the week before.

"I still can't believe this is happening." Charlotte's face was streaked with white paint from the roller she was using to on the walls in her new art gallery. "I always dreamed of showing my paintings here in Candle Beach, but after the previous tenant left before I could do it, I thought I was out of luck."

"And now *you're* the gallery owner." Amelia smiled at her friend. She was pretty sure her own face was glowing as much as Charlotte's. Her half of the space was prepped for painting and she'd already installed shelves in her office. They'd be perfect for housing the interior design samples she'd arranged to be shipped from her storage unit in San Francisco. "Things are really coming together around here."

She still couldn't quite understand how her life had turned around so quickly. Only a month ago, she'd been unhappy at the hotel and wondering how she'd get through each day. Now she was the proud owner of an interior design business and was dating a movie star. Although Jordan had taken the movie role when it was offered, he was making an effort to stay in touch with her as much as possible. The night before, she'd had a video chat with both him and Mia as she advised him on a craft project he was doing with his daughter.

She eyed the wall clock they'd set on the counter while the walls were being painted. "We'd better get cleaned up soon. I don't want to be the last person to Dahlia's house."

"Ooh," Charlotte's face lit up. "You're right. I'm so excited to see her baby!" She washed off her paintbrush and set it carefully on a newspaper to dry before rushing off to the bathroom to get cleaned up.

Dahlia had given birth a week ago, but as a new mom, she'd requested that her friends wait until she'd had a little time to adjust to the huge life change. Her husband Garrett and mother-in-law Wendy were hosting a get-together at Dahlia's house where all of her friends could meet the baby at the same time.

"What do you think she named him?" Amelia asked as they walked up the hill to Dahlia's house.

"Last I heard, it was a toss-up between John and Matthew." Charlotte skipped a little, making Amelia laugh. "Sorry, I'm just so happy. My friends are having babies and I might be getting married..."

Amelia stopped mid-step. "Wait, what? Did you say you were getting married?"

Charlotte blushed. "Luke and I have been talking about it. Nothing official yet, but maybe next summer. He asked me what kind of ring I'd like." She giggled. "Good thing because I'm pretty picky about jewelry."

Amelia threw her arms around Charlotte. "I'm so happy for you." In the past if she'd said something like that, she would have meant it, but a little part of herself would have died inside from jealousy. Now that she was happily in a serious relationship with Jordan, she truly meant it.

"Thanks. But don't say anything to anyone at the party. This is Dahlia's big day."

Amelia moved her fingers across her lips. "My lips are zipped."

They walked the remaining few blocks to Dahlia's house, a grand old Craftsman that sat at the top of the hill, overlooking the Pacific Ocean and all of town.

"I love how many different ways there are here to experience the ocean," Amelia said. "It looks so different from Dahlia's house than it does from the beach, or even up on the cliff near the hotel."

"Me too. It's always beautiful, but ever-changing. That's why I love painting the local area so much." Charlotte walked up the front steps to Dahlia and Garrett's porch and knocked on the door. No one answered, so she pushed the door open.

In the living room, everyone was gathered around Dahlia, who was sitting in a rocking chair, holding a little baby with a full shock of dark brown hair.

Gretchen waved excitedly at them. "Come in! Dahlia just got down here, and she was about to introduce us to the baby."

Amelia and Charlotte moved closer to the group.

Dahlia looked up at them. "Girls, meet our new son, Jonathan Edward Callahan – Johnny for short."

Dahlia's mother beamed. "It seems fitting that another Edward is living in this house. I have such fond memories of living here with Aunt Ruth and Uncle Ed."

Dahlia smiled at her mother. "If it weren't for Aunt Ruth giving me this house and bringing me back to Candle Beach, I wouldn't be here with Garrett, or be the mother of this little one." Pure joy filled her face as she gazed down at her son.

"He's so handsome, Dahlia," Amelia said.

"Any chance you'll let us hold him?" Charlotte asked, her eyes gleaming.

Dahlia grinned at her. "I think I see him enough. You can spend some time with him." She held her blanket-wrapped son up to Charlotte, who rushed to grab him.

Charlotte snuggled him to her chest, kissing his head. "He's got that new baby smell."

"Is that kind of like a new car smell?" Gretchen teased.

"Kind of, but better." Charlotte smirked at her. "When are you and Parker going to give me a new niece or nephew anyway?"

Gretchen laughed. "Maybe next year." She paused. "Now that things are getting more settled with our real estate company, we've talked a little about starting a family."

Charlotte squealed. "Ooh!" The baby's eyes popped open and Charlotte whispered to him, "Sorry, Johnny." She rocked him until he fell back asleep.

"Looks like Maggie and I have started a trend." Dahlia leaned back in her chair. "A warning to you though – having a baby is no joke. I don't think I've slept more than two hours at a time since he was born."

Garrett came out of the kitchen and heard his wife talking. "Hey, I fed him last night."

"Yeah, but I still woke up when I heard him crying." She sighed, then smiled at him. "But thank you."

"It'll get better in a month or two when he starts sleeping for longer periods of time," Dahlia's mother said. "Just enjoy this time for what it is."

"I'll try to remember that through my lack-of-sleep-addled brain." Dahlia settled into the pillows on her chair and closed her eyes.

The front door opened, and Maggie entered, carrying her baby, whom they'd decided to name Lizzie. "I heard this was a baby party, so I brought one more."

Maura and their other friends, Angel and Sarah followed her in, carrying a diaper bag and a portable bassinet.

"All of that for a visit?" Garrett asked, his eyes wide.

Maggie laughed. "Oh, you'll learn. When you leave the house, you practically have to carry everything but the kitchen sink."

He looked at her with skepticism, but his mom and mother-in-law exchanged amused glances.

"Oh honey, you'll see when you take the baby out," Wendy said, patting his arm. He just shook his head and returned to the safety of the kitchen, where some of the husbands were gathered.

"How is our little Lizzie?" Amelia asked.

"Sleepy, as usual." Maggie held her out to Amelia. "Want to hold her?"

Amelia nodded. She may not have been as baby crazy as Charlotte, but she wasn't going to turn down a chance to hold Maggie's little girl. She carefully took Lizzie from Maggie and held her close. The baby looked up and Amelia could swear she smiled at her. She sat down with Sarah on the couch, snuggling Lizzie and listening to her friends catch up on each other's busy lives. Dahlia had fallen asleep in her rocker and she snored softly as everyone chattered around her. Gretchen grabbed a pillow off a nearby chair and propped it behind Dahlia's head, then sat down beside Amelia to admire the baby too.

Amelia felt warm and happy. She'd had friends in the Bay Area, but nothing compared to the closeness she'd already developed with this group of friends. She wanted to stay a part of this community for a long time and hoped to raise her own children here in Candle Beach. She didn't know yet whether Jordan would decide to move up to Washington, and although she didn't want to influence his decision, she really hoped he would. He had to be a part of her future, whether that was in Candle Beach or wherever he was living. Whatever happened, she was sure things would work out, and the women gathered around her would be her friends for life.

~

That evening, a knock sounded on the door to Amelia's cottage and she ran to open it.

"Pizza delivery," Jordan sang out as he handed her the large pepperoni pizza she'd ordered from Pete's Pizza. "I caught the delivery guy in the hotel lobby, asking for you."

"I'm so glad the pizza is finally here. I'm starving." She grabbed it from him and turned around rapidly.

He caught her around the waist. "What am I, chopped liver?"

"Oh, okay. I'm glad you're finally here too." She grinned impishly at him, set the pizza on the coffee table, and wrapped her arms around his neck. "I can't believe you got the weekend off from filming."

He shrugged. "I negotiated my contract well. Being the star has its benefits. Some celebrities ask for fancy bottled water and caviar in their dressing room – I asked for two weekends off and two nights a week free so that I could spend time with you and Mia." He leaned down and kissed her. "I think I got the better deal."

"Well, I'm certainly glad you did. But really, I am starving." She reached for the pizza, then noticed he was holding a small bag. "What's that?"

"You said you hadn't seen any of my movies, so I brought

one of the most recent I was in, and something else that I know you'll love." He dipped his hand into the bag and pulled out the black-and-white movie that she'd been hunting for on eBay.

She gasped, plucking the movie out of his hands. "Daisy's Choice? Where did you find that? I've been looking for this movie for a year."

He gave her a mysterious smile. "Being in showbiz has its perks. I had someone track it down for me."

"Hmm," she said. "I could get used to dating a celebrity."

An expression of mock horror came over his face. "You'd better. I don't intend to go anywhere." He sat down on the couch.

She sighed dramatically. "Then I guess I'll have to get used to it." She eyed the old movie. "Can we watch this one?"

"What? You don't want to watch my acting? I'm not too bad, I swear."

"Uh, I already saw it." In the last two weeks, she'd watched most of his movies. Even though he was pretending to be someone else on screen, it still felt like a part of him was there with her. And he was right, he wasn't too bad of an actor, as well as being easy on the eyes.

A self-satisfied smile stretched across his lips. "You did? You missed me, didn't you?"

"I did." She slid the DVD of the old movie into the player, then sat on the couch and snuggled up to him. "Seeing your movies helped, but I'm really glad you're here in person now."

"Me too." He wrapped his arm around her shoulders, pulling her closer.

The movie started and Amelia let herself relax against him, feeling his warm embrace. Her own life was starting to feel like a romantic movie, and she couldn't wait to see what happened in the next act.

~

Author's Note

Thank you for reading Sweet Sacrifices. If this is your first Candle Beach novel, check out the rest of the series to read about Amelia's friends as they find love in unexpected places. If you're a fan of cozy mysteries, try out my Jill Andrews Cozy Mystery series. Happy reading!

Candle Beach Novels

Sweet Beginnings (Book 1)
Sweet Success (Book 2)
Sweet Promises (Book 3)
Sweet Memories (Book 4)
Sweet History (Book 5)
Sweet Matchmaking (Book 6)
Sweet Surprises (Book 7)
Sweet Sacrifices (Book 8)

Jill Andrews Cozy Mysteries

Brownie Points for Murder (Book 1)
Death to the Highest Bidder (Book 2)
A Deadly Pair O'Docks (Book 3)
Stuck with S'More Death (Book 4)
Murderous Mummy Wars (Book 5)
A Killer Christmas Party (Book 6)

<<<<>>>>

ACKNOWLEDGMENTS

Cover Design: Elizabeth Mackey Graphic Design

Made in the USA
Middletown, DE
03 March 2021

34705201R00104